PUFFIN BOOKS

SUPER GRAN RULES OK!

Watch out for Super Gran, the old lady with incredible strength, fantastic speed and X-ray eyes! She's back again, this time defending an amazing new invention — the Skimmer — from the attentions of both a band of small-time crooks *and* the government's Department Y.

Why Department Y? Read on to find the answer, and to learn how Super Gran overcomes her failing powers and, with the help of her young friends Edison, Willard and Tub, deals a terrible blow at the forces of evil.

Forrest Wilson's marvellously comic heroine stars again in a book that will amuse and entertain readers of nine and over.

Forrest Wilson

SUPER GRAN RULES OK!

Illustrated by David McKee

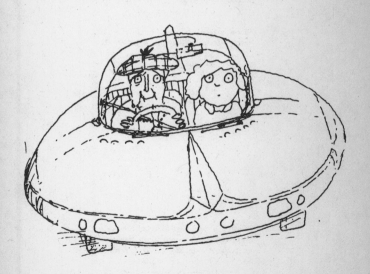

PUFFIN BOOKS

To Jean and Eunice

Puffin Books, Penguin Books Ltd, Harmondsworth, Middlesex, England
Penguin Books, 625 Madison Avenue, New York, New York 10022, U.S.A.
Penguin Books Australia Ltd, Ringwood, Victoria, Australia
Penguin Books Canada Ltd, 2801 John Street, Markham, Ontario, Canada L3R 1B4
Penguin Books (N.Z.) Ltd, 182–190 Wairau Road, Auckland 10, New Zealand

First published 1981

Filmset, printed and bound in Great Britain by
Hazell Watson & Viney Ltd, Aylesbury, Bucks
Set in V.I.P. Garamond

Contents

1 Canal Capers

'Look out, Willie — the canal . . .!' Super Gran yelled, as she Super-sprinted across the uneven cobblestones of the towpath towards the boy, her grandson Willard, to save him from a watery grave.

Super Gran, on her way to meet and play football with Willard (after he had coaxed and nagged her to have a proper, full-length game with him), had spotted him, a few hundred metres away, approaching her along the canal bank.

The trouble was, Willard was not content merely to *walk* along the canal path. That was too boring, too tame and a complete waste of time to the boy, who was football mad. So he had been dribbling the ball along, kicking it against the wall at the side of the path, 'trapping' it underfoot on the rebound, tackling an imaginary opponent and doing a fancy piece of head-and-chest ball-juggling (which Super Gran remembered was called 'keepie-uppie' in her young days in Scotland).

But then Super Gran, walking sedately towards him, her handbag slung over her arm, saw that Willard was dribbling the ball right at the very edge of the canal. He didn't have much room . . . He was taking a step sideways . . . Then . . .

'Look out, Willie . . .!'

As Super Gran sped along, Willard lost his balance and, complete with football, he toppled over the edge, right into the canal's murky waters. She dived forward, making a grab for him. She caught him by the collar as he went under, and she yanked him, in one straight pull, from the dirty depths of the waterway on to the safety of the towpath.

'Whew, laddie, that was a near thing!' she cried. 'Just as well your poor, weak, little old grannie was here to rescue you, wasn't it?'

A poor, weak, little old grannie – was what Super Gran was *not*!

'Crumbs! Thanks, Gran,' Willard spluttered. Then he pointed to where his football, now imitating a water-polo ball, was intent on reaching the canal's far bank. 'My ball, Gran! It's floatin' away! Can you get it?'

'Your *ball*?' Super Gran shook her head. 'Is that all that's bothering you, laddie? And you just an inch away from a watery grave?'

'I was *not*!' Willard denied, indignantly. 'I could easily have climbed out again if you hadn't been there . . .'

'Oh, you could, could you?' Super Gran pretended to scowl. 'Right then, sonny, I'll just push you back in and we'll see, shall we . . .?'

'No! No, Gran!' Willard put his hand out, to stop her carrying out her threat. 'I was only kiddin'! Honest!'

'Aye! And I should think so too,' Super Gran murmured. 'That's all the thanks I get for rescuing you. Humph!' She pretended to be huffed.

'Tell you what, Gran,' Willard beamed, as he climbed to his feet, soaking wet, and squelched about from one foot to the other, 'I'll really thank you — *if* you rescue my ball too!' He pointed to where it had come to rest at the far bank.

'Huh! That's easy-peasy!' Super Gran exclaimed. 'But I suppose I'd better just take a wee bit of a run at it. In case I don't manage a standing jump, eh?'

She paced back about a dozen metres along the length of the towpath, and then, racing forward, she launched herself into space — and clear over the canal!

Although Willard was used to seeing his Gran performing her Super-feats, he still held his breath until she landed safely on the path on the other side. Just in case!

Super Gran landed, picked the ball out of the water, paced back along the canal, ran, leapt — and landed back beside Willard again. Just like that! And with her handbag still slung over her arm!

She handed Willard the ball and they set off, Willard squelching at every step, to go home. He was too wet now to think about playing football.

'Och, don't worry,' Super Gran said, 'we'll have a wee game another time, eh?'

They walked a few hundred metres along the path until a bend in the canal brought them to a lock, which would have provided them with a bridge to cross the water. Willard pointed to it.

'Look Gran, I forgot about that. You needn't have bothered jumpin' over. You could've crossed there.'

Super Gran grinned hugely. 'Aye, you're right, Willie. But it was more fun my way, wasn't it?'

They left the canal and headed towards the main road, where they met Edison Black, the girl who had shared their earlier adventure, when Super Gran had *become* Super Gran.

'What on earth's happened to you?' the girl asked the sodden, dripping Willard.

'Mind your own business!' Willard retorted, scowling.

'You look as if you've fallen into the canal!' Edison laughed.

'He *has* just fallen into the canal!' Super Gran told her. 'I had to yank him out!'

Willard turned his scowl in his Gran's direction. He hadn't wanted Super Gran to tell anyone what had happened, and especially not Edison. For Edison was just about his least favourite acquaintance, tending to take up too much of his Gran's time; time which Willard wanted for himself.

'Huh! Trust *you*!' Edison said, scornfully. 'What were you doing there? Playing *foot*ball again, I shouldn't wonder!'

'What's wrong with football?'

'I knew it. Trip over your feet, did you?'

'Huh! Listen to who's talkin' about trippin' over their feet!' Willard was aghast. 'Huh! *You* can't even *walk* without trippin' over yours!'

'I can so!' Edison retorted, haughtily; then spoiled the effect — by tripping over her feet!

Willard guffawed. 'See? What'd I tell you?'

'All right, silly Willie . . .!'

Willard didn't like being called that. 'All right, Ginger!' he taunted, referring to Edison's hair.

'It isn't ginger, it's auburn!' she replied, making a face.

Super Gran decided that their slanging match had gone on long enough. 'Right, that does it,' she said, grabbing each of them by a shoulder and making as if to bang their heads together.

'No, Super Gran . . .'

'Don't, Gran . . .'

'Stop . . .!' they both pleaded, terrified. They knew that if Super Gran were to carry out her threat, her Super-strength was enough to knock their heads right off their shoulders!

Luckily, she was only pretending, to bring them to their senses. And it worked. For that was the end of the argument, although they scowled at each other for another five minutes until their tempers cooled.

'I've got an awful job with you two, so I have,' Super Gran murmured, shaking her head.

Edison glanced across at the soaking-wet Willard, looking him up and down from his hair, plastered down over his head, to his squelchy shoes and the sodden clothes in between. 'What'll your Mum say?'

Willard looked down at himself, seeing the wet canal mud which covered him and realizing just what a mess he was in. 'Cr-umbs! She'll kill me!' he muttered.

'I'll bet she will,' said a hopeful Edison, trying to hide a smile. She sniggered, but hastily turned it into a cough when Willard scowled at her again. She didn't want to push her luck too far. She was happy to see him getting into trouble, but she didn't want to start another war of words with him and risk Super Gran's wrath.

'She'll kill me!' Willard repeated.

Edison put on what she imagined was a grown-up 'face' and mimicked: 'Don't you dare come home drowned — or I'll kill you . . .!'

The unintentional humour of Edison's statement dawned on all three of them — and they ended up laughing instead of fighting. For once!

'You'd better get out of those wet clothes,' Super Gran said.

'What — here? In the middle of the street?' Willard gasped.

'No, not exactly, laddie!' Super Gran laughed.

'Why don't you come to *my* house,' Edison suggested. 'It's nearest. And Willard could put on some of Dad's clothes, while his dry.'

'Aye, and I've got an even better idea,' Super Gran said. 'I'll blow them dry. With my breath!'

'*Could* you, Gran?' Willard asked.

'Of *course* I could,' Super Gran assured him. 'You should know by this time — I can do *any*thing!'

They hurried to Edison's house and borrowed a shirt and a pair of trousers for Willard to wear, while Super Gran took his wet, muddy discarded clothes into the back garden, hung them on the clothesline and blew them dry, with her Super-breath.

'Just look at you in my Dad's clothes!' Edison

giggled. The shirt sleeves were far too long for Willard's arms and the trouser legs kept tripping him up when he walked. 'They're so big — they "drown" you!' She laughed, and explained, 'First of all he nearly drowned in the canal — and now he's *drowned* in Dad's clothes!'

Edison, too busy laughing at her own joke, made the mistake of wandering in front of the clothesline on which Willard's clothes were hanging, and, therefore, in front of Super Gran's Super-breath, which was drying them. With the result that the Super-blast knocked her off her feet and sent her sprawling a dozen metres across the garden — until she ended up against the garden shed, her father's workshop.

'Ow! Ouch!' she gasped — *after* she had got her breath back, minutes later. And *after* Willard had howled with laughter at her predicament.

She glared at the boy as she struggled to her feet, and was just about to give him a piece of her mind when her father came in through the garden gate in his wheelchair, and wheeled it round the corner of the house towards them.

'Hi, Dad. Where've you been?' Edison greeted him.

'Oh, hello folks. I've just been along at my friend Mr Decker's place, to use some of the power-tools in his little factory.'

Edison explained to the other two that her father's workshop, the garden shed, was not equipped with all the tools that he needed for building his various inventions.

'Oh, that reminds me,' Super Gran said, turning her attention from Willard's now-dry (but still muddy!)

clothes to the man in the wheelchair. 'Talking about inventions . . .!'

Mr Black didn't need Super Gran's mind-reading Super-powers to know what was coming next! For she hadn't stopped nagging him about it since the last one had been destroyed. 'The Super-machine . . .?'

'The Super-machine! Aye, you're right. When are you going to build me a new one, eh? It's weeks now since yon last one blew up.'

'Oh . . . ah . . . well, you see . . .' Mr Black tried to think of an excuse. A *new* excuse, that was! For he had already made a dozen excuses for why he had not, as yet, started work on rebuilding the machine which had made Super Gran Super in the first place, and which had blown up, afterwards.

The truth of the matter was that Mr Black couldn't be bothered returning to his *old* inventions again. He was only interested in *new* inventions. As soon as he had invented something – he lost interest in it. But when he explained this to Super Gran, she wouldn't listen to him; she just wanted another one built – right away!

She wasn't a nag, as a rule. But in the case of the Super-machine – she made an exception to the rule!

'It's not as if you haven't got the money to build a new one,' she went on, as Edison, having heard the argument before, slipped into the house to make a cup of tea.

Mr Black nodded, guiltily. Again, he knew what was coming!

'After all,' Super Gran continued, frowning, 'I gave

you most of the reward money I got for catching yon bank-robbers, didn't I?'

He nodded again. She certainly had given him the money (keeping only a small amount, in her bank, for a 'rainy day') — but he kept using it for tools and materials for his *new* inventions, instead of for materials for rebuilding the old Super-machine. 'Well, you see . . . ah . . .'

'And you know *why* I want the Super-machine, don't you?' she asked.

He knew that as well. But she told him, anyway!

'So that I can turn all my old friends into Super-Oldies, like myself. All the old folk in town. And then, afterwards, the old folk in the whole country.'

'Ah well, you see . . . um . . . ah . . . it's like this . . . ah . . .' he began. But just then Edison popped her head out of the back door, to announce: 'Tea's up!'

'Oh? Tea? Oh, good,' Mr Black smiled, as he wheeled his chair vigorously towards the ramp leading to the door, feeling that, like a battered, bruised boxer, he had been 'saved by the bell'! 'Tea? Good, I'm starving. Starving!'

2   The Skimmer

While they sat watching television after tea, Mr Black's thoughts were still on Super Gran and the Super-machine.

He really *should* make a start on rebuilding it, he scolded himself. She *had* given him the money, after all. He had no excuse, really. He *would* do it, *some* day — but not just yet! Meantime, there were plenty of other things he wanted to invent.

He paused, and asked himself, like what, for instance? Well, like . . . like . . . He couldn't think of anything, not just at that moment. But he would. Given time.

He was suddenly wakened out of his day-dream by a shout from Willard, who was pointing to the television screen, impressed by something he had been watching. Edison's father looked at it, dragging his mind back from his inventions, past and future. He saw that it was one of those cartoon series set in space, full of spaceships, aliens, invaders, ray-guns, lasers, time-warps — and all the usual Science Fiction gimmicks.

His attention was caught by a space vehicle which seemed to be having a large piece of the action just then. Like a flying saucer in shape, it could travel on roads like a car, on the sea like a boat, and in the air like an aircraft. In fact, it seemed able to do just about *any*thing! An extremely versatile vehicle!

If only someone were to invent something like that *now*, he thought, instead of in the future. An *actual* craft like that, instead of just a TV cartoon one . . .

As he watched the craft, full of 'baddies', zoom down out of the sky to chase the 'goodies', and he saw it skim low over houses, hedges and bridges, he decided that *that* would be his next invention. And he would call it a 'Skimmer' (because it skimmed!).

Thinking that he was thinking to himself, and not realizing that he was speaking out loud, he exclaimed excitedly, 'That's it! I'm going to make a start on it! Right now! This very minute!'

He swung his chair to one side and then, guiding its wheels between the other furniture, he left the room, heading for his workshop.

'Did you hear that?' Super Gran cried, 'he's going to make a start on it — right now!'

'What's that, Gran?' Willard wasn't really listening. He was too engrossed in whether the TV cartoon's 'goodies' would outrun the 'baddies'.

'The machine,' Super Gran explained, 'the Super-machine . . .' She turned to Edison, who gave her more attention than Willard had done. 'Your Dad — that's him off to make a start on rebuilding the Super-machine. Isn't that good?'

'Yes, Super Gran,' Edison agreed, 'that's good. Great!'

The three of them settled down to give their whole

attention to the cartoon on the television once more.

If only Super Gran had tuned her mind-reading powers in on Mr Black — she would have known better! But, of course, she had no cause to.

However, a couple of weeks later she found out her mistake!

Edison had been sent by her father round to Super Gran's house, to fetch her along to Mr Decker's little factory. When she arrived, she found Super Gran at her breakfast.

'Ooooooh, porridge . . .!' Edison made a face. 'I don't fancy porridge much.'

'M'mm,' Super Gran enthused. 'I have it every morning. Couldn't do without it!'

Edison suddenly remembered her mission. 'Never mind that, Super Gran. Dad's got a surprise for you. Round at Mr Decker's place.'

'M'mm,' said Super Gran again, between mouthfuls, 'and *I've* got a surprise for *you* too.' She grinned hugely, obviously pleased with herself. 'I got a letter this morning, from a Mr Silver. He's organizing the "Modern Times" exhibition, up in London. And what d'you think . . .?'

'What?'

'He wants me to go up there next week, to demonstrate my Super-powers. At the exhibition!'

'Oh, Super Gran, that's great,' Edison exclaimed, pleased with her old friend's good news.

'And there'll be crowds of newspaper reporters and radio and TV people there,' Super Gran went on, 'so I'll get lots of publicity, and become *really* famous. They'll hear about me all over the country. Not just here in Chisleton.'

Edison was delighted. 'Oh yes, you *will* become famous. And you'll maybe get on the telly . . .?'

'*And* I've to get all my expenses paid,' Super Gran beamed. 'And stay in one of yon posh hotels, up there . . .!'

'Oh, Super Gran . . .!'

'And he said I could take a friend with me,' she went on. 'But I thought I'd rather take two *half*-friends, instead!' She paused and looked at the puzzled girl, adding: 'You and Willard, of course!'

'*Half*-friends . . .?' It took Edison a moment to figure out that two children equalled one adult, more or less, where hotel expenses and railway fares and so on were concerned. 'Oh yes, I see *now* what you mean. And we can go with you? Really?' Her smile was six metres wide. 'Oh, that's super, Super Gran!' She laughed.

Then she suddenly remembered her mission – again! 'Oh, I'm forgetting all about Dad's surprise. I'm supposed to be fetching you along to Mr Decker's factory. We'd better hurry.'

'What *is* the surprise?' Super Gran asked, when she had cleared up the breakfast things and they were hurrying along through the back-streets of the town towards the factory, across the road from the town's public park. 'Oh, *I* know! It's the Super-machine, isn't it? He's built a new one, hasn't he? It's ready?'

'I dunno, Super Gran. Honestly,' Edison said. 'He just told me to fetch you along there.' Then she added:

'I was supposed to bring Willard along too. But his Mum says he's out playing football somewhere.' She sniffed, disdainfully. 'He *always* is.'

They reached the little factory, to be met by Mr Black, in his wheelchair, in the yard at the back, talking to a large, purple-faced man, beside whom stood an object covered by a large white tarpaulin.

'Ah! Here they are,' Mr Black said, and introduced her to the man. 'Super Gran, this is my friend, Mr Decker . . .'

'More like "double Decker", eh?' the man interrupted, guffawing and slapping his rather stout stomach.

'He lets me use his factory sometimes,' Mr Black went on. 'And . . .'

'What he means,' Mr Decker interrupted again, 'is that *he* lets *me* — or rather, *us* — build his confounded inventions here for him!' The large, jovial man boomed heartily. 'Still, we do make a good team, don't we, Black?' He turned to Super Gran and Edison. 'You've heard of us, haven't you? Black — and Decker, eh? What? Ha, ha!' He guffawed again, his double chin vibrating like a piano accordion, with laughter. 'You know the "drill", don't you? Ha, ha — the "drill" — get it? Black and Decker — "drill" . . .?' He laughed even more uproariously and his laughter was infectious. The others all joined in. They couldn't help themselves!

'You see,' Edison's father explained to Super Gran, 'sometimes I can't manage to build my inventions by myself. I need help. I can't get my wheelchair around some of the gadgets and, in this case, I couldn't get it *in*side, to work on the controls, and so I . . .' As he said this, his hand was on the edge of the tarpaulin, ready to pull it off and reveal the mysterious object hiding under it.

'What d'you mean "*in*side it"?' Super Gran asked, puzzled. 'You don't need to get *inside* the Super-machine! You can't *get* inside the Super-machine!' She decided to turn her X-ray eyesight on to the sheeted object, to see what was under the sheet – but before she could do so, Mr Black had whipped the cover off, to reveal . . .

'The Skimmer!' he announced, proudly.

'What in the name's that?' the old lady exclaimed, taken aback at seeing the craft, which looked like a flying saucer on wheels – when she had expected to see a rebuilt Super-machine, a completely different-shaped gadget altogether. Although, funnily enough, she thought there was something familiar about it.

'Er . . . ah . . . this . . . this is my new invention, Super Gran,' Mr Black confessed, apologetically. 'I call it a "Skimmer".'

'And *I* call it a con-trick! And I call *you* a fraud! Not to mention – a wee scunner and a wee bachle and a wee . . .' She stopped for a breath, then continued: 'You got me round here on false pretences. You said I was to come and see the surprise you had for me – the Super-machine . . .'

'I didn't mention Super-machine!'

'No, he didn't say that, Super Gran,' Edison confirmed. 'He just said he had a surprise for you.'

'Well, it's a surprise for me all right, I'll say that.

22

But what happened to the Super-machine? You distinctly said you were going to start work on it right away.'

'What? Me?' It was Mr Black's turn to look puzzled. 'When did I say *that*?'

'The day we were round at your house watching television. Watching yon space cartoon thing, with all yon space gadgets and aliens and spaceships and . . .' It suddenly dawned on Super Gran that what she was looking at was the vehicle she had seen on TV. So *that* was why it seemed familiar!

She turned to look from Mr Black, who was grinning hugely, to Mr Decker, who was also grinning hugely and was nodding his head, as if to say: 'Yes, it *is* the vehicle you saw on TV!'

She looked at Edison, who shrugged, as if to say: 'Don't blame *me*! *I* didn't know what was going on!'

Slowly Super Gran grinned as a thought came to her. She recalled that the TV version had been capable of doing all sorts of things. It could float and fly, it could hover and swoop and zoom and skim about.

'Can it do what the telly one could do?' she asked. Mr Black nodded. 'Can it float? And fly?'

Mr Black nodded vigorously. 'It sure can,' he beamed proudly, turning to Mr Decker, 'can't it?'

'It certainly can,' his friend grinned. 'I've had a go at it. It's great. The only thing is, I don't know whether you'd need a driving licence, a ship's captain's licence – or a pilot's licence!' He guffawed again.

'Can *I* have a shot?' Super Gran asked, her annoyance at Mr Black's deception forgotten. After all, the Super-machine could be rebuilt some other time. In the *mean*time, there was a great new invention — a brand new type of 'super' vehicle — to be tried out! The Super-machine could wait. The Skimmer couldn't!

She approached it and looked through the glass-dome roof at the controls, inside the cab. 'Is it easy to operate?'

Mr Decker, smiling, came forward. 'I'll show you.'

Mr Black, pleased with the interest that Super Gran was showing in it, breathed a sigh of relief that her annoyance about the Super-machine had evaporated. For the time being!

'You see,' Mr Decker explained, 'as Mr Black can't get in and out of the Skimmer, I — and my workmen, of course — did the actual work on it. The *hard* work! All *he* did,' he nodded towards his partner, 'was design it.'

He showed Super Gran and Edison the details of the new craft. He demonstrated how to open the glass-dome roof and how to climb up and inside the cab; where the various controls were; which switch operated the 'car' controls, which levers operated the 'boat' controls and which pedals and handles operated the 'aircraft' controls.

The vehicle itself was the size of a mini-car, was circular in shape, could carry four people and had adjustable, reclining seats. It had four wheels, small retractable wings and a little tail-plane assembly. There was also a retractable outboard motor at the rear, for propelling it through water, and underneath it had a downward-thrusting jet engine, for making it fly.

(Although, as Mr Black pointed out, it was really more like hovering than flying, as at present it would lift off the ground only about ten metres. But he assured them that he was working on ways of making it go higher!)

'And then there's the anti-theft device,' he added, explaining that the Skimmer would operate only when the steering wheel was in the 'out' position, away from the dashboard; that a specially strong spring held it, otherwise, against the board. And to unlock this spring and release the steering wheel, a special key was needed.

'And without the key,' he told them, 'you've had it! The Skimmer just won't work!'

'Not unless Super Gran can *pull* the wheel out,' Edison suggested.

'M'mm, that's possible,' her father admitted. 'But she'd be so busy holding it out that she wouldn't be able to operate the controls at the same time. No, the spring's so strong that I'm sure it's completely thief-proof.'

'Can we take it for a test-drive?' Super Gran asked eagerly, her eyes gleaming.

'Sure thing,' Mr Black replied. 'The ignition key is built into the switch. But here's the other one – for the anti-theft device.' He threw her a key, adding: 'And don't lose it, it's the only one I've got.'

'You should've made a duplicate key, Dad,' Edison pointed out, 'in case it gets lost.'

'Yes, I'll do that some time,' Mr Black said, vaguely.

'Aye, at the same time you're rebuilding my Super-machine, no doubt!' Super Gran retorted.

'Shouldn't we call this a test-"skim", instead of a test-drive?' Edison commented, as she and Super Gran climbed up inside the craft.

After a few minutes of tuition from Mr Decker, Super Gran unlocked the anti-theft device, switched on the ignition, put the Skimmer into gear, let out the clutch, closed down the dome roof — and began to steer the vehicle slowly out of the factory yard, watched proudly by Mr Black and Mr Decker.

But they all — all four of them — forgot one thing. They forgot that, although Super Gran could learn to drive, sail and fly the Skimmer after only a few minutes' tuition (which she could do, with her Super-powers), she did not have a driving licence . . . and she was liable to get into trouble for breaking the law!

3   The Vulgar Boatman!

'Oh, I forgot,' said Mr Black, the typical absent-minded inventor, a few seconds later, 'she probably doesn't have a driving licence. *And* the Skimmer's not road-taxed! *And* it's not insured! *And* it's got no number plates! But apart from that — it's all right!'

'*Now* you tell me!' sighed his friend, his grin fading momentarily.

'And I meant to tell her just to take it for a spin in the park, across the street there, and *not* on the main roads,' Mr Black went on. 'But I forgot. I hope she thinks of it herself. Or maybe Edison'll think of it. She usually thinks of those sorts of things.'

(What he really meant was: 'Edison is a bit of a nag! She's always keeping *me* on the right lines!')

But neither Super Gran *nor* the usually efficient Edison *did* think about it. For they were both too busy enjoying themselves on their test-'skim'.

At first they drove the craft along the main road alongside the factory, slowly and steadily, but, as Super Gran's confidence grew, so their speed increased, until Edison began to worry.

'Slow down, Super Gran,' she frowned, 'you're going too fast. *And* it's zig-zagging all over the road!'

'Havers, lassie! I'm not doing so bad, for my first attempt at driving!'

But the young, sour-faced policeman who approached them, on his beat, thought the same as Edison. *And*, he thought, there's something peculiar about that flying saucer that's coming along the road towards me erratically . . . Hey! A flying saucer? he thought — suddenly realizing that a flying saucer had no right to be travelling along *any* public road — never mind a public road on *his* beat!

His mouth dropped open in disbelief. Then it dropped even further open when he saw that there was a little old lady at the controls! And, by the look of it, it was obviously her very first attempt at driving a car. Not that it *was* a car — or was it? It certainly moved like a car — but it looked like a flying saucer!

As it reached him, the policeman spotted that the Skimmer had no number plates. 'Ah! Got you!' he muttered, whipping out his notebook and pencil to note its number — before remembering that it didn't *have* a number for him to note! 'Humph! I'll bet she's breaking another dozen laws as well!'

He waved his arms at them to stop; he jumped up and down; he blew his police whistle at them — but Super Gran, as the Skimmer passed by, just ignored him.

'Super Gran, that was a policeman waving at us to stop,' a worried Edison murmured, looking back to see the jumping, whistle-blowing, notebook-waving young constable on the pavement.

'What? A policeman?' Super Gran remarked casually. 'Oh? I didn't notice him. I must be getting old!'

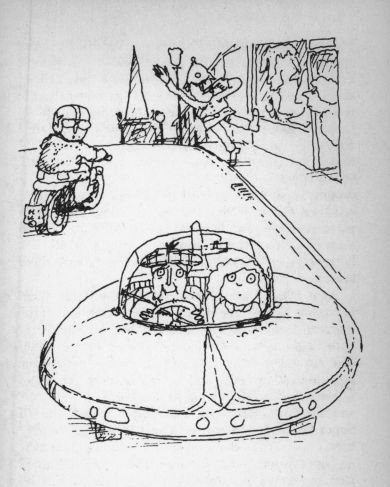

She smiled, fibbing, and hastily swerved the Skimmer in through the gates of the public park.

As Edison hadn't been prepared for this sudden swerve, and as she hadn't fastened her seat-belt, she banged her head on the inside of the dome. 'Ouch!'

'Sorry about that,' Super Gran apologized, 'but I *had* to get away from that policeman . . . er . . . I mean, not that I *saw* a policeman, you understand!' She laughed.

'Oh, Super Gran, you *are* awful!' Edison giggled.

Super Gran steered the vehicle along the main pathway in the park, between two stretches of grass, on one of which a group of boys was playing football.

'Look, there's Willard,' Edison pointed, 'with those boys.'

Super Gran headed the Skimmer towards them until, one by one, the boys took their attention off the game to look their way. The last one to spot them, being the one who was most engrossed in the game, was, of course, Willard. But finally even *he* noticed the strange-looking craft, and he ran from the crowd of gaping boys on recognizing its occupants.

'Gran!' he called out, excitedly, 'What's this? I didn't know *you* could drive! Can *I* have a ride in it?'

She opened the dome roof. 'It's Edison's Dad's new invention, it's called a Skimmer, I've only just learned to drive and yes, certainly, come for a drive. Climb in!'

Willard climbed up the footholds on the chassis and jumped into the cab. 'Move over, Red!' he ordered, trying to push Edison aside to get into the front passenger seat beside Super Gran.

'Move over yourself, Willie!' Edison retorted, shoving him roughly into one of the back seats.

'Now then, you two, don't start *that* again!' Super Gran closed the roof, glanced in the rear-view mirror and exclaimed: 'Oh-oh!'

'What is it, Super Gran?' Edison turned round in her seat. 'Oh, it's that policeman. He's followed us!'

'We'd better get moving,' the old lady said, as she let the clutch out and the Skimmer shot off again, faster this time.

'But what *is* it?' Willard asked. 'It looks like a flyin' saucer, or somethin'! *Is* it a car? It's a funny-looking car, if it is! And what's that thing at the back for? It looks like an aeroplane!'

'Well, it is, sort of,' Edison explained. 'It can float like a boat, and . . .'

'A boat?' Willard exclaimed, interrupting. 'Let's try it out on the boatin'-lake, then.'

'Good idea, laddie!' his Gran agreed. 'We haven't tried it out as a boat yet. *Nor* as a plane.'

'A plane?' Willard gasped. 'A plane? You mean — this thing can *fly*?'

'Well, it's supposed to,' Super Gran said, 'but we haven't tried it yet. Edison's father says it can fly, though.'

'And if he *says* it can, then it can!' Edison defended him, thinking that the others didn't believe her father's claims.

Super Gran, meanwhile, had been operating the Skimmer's hovering controls (by moving a handle which gave the machine a small amount of upward thrust, lifting it a few centimetres off the grass) — making it skim and giving it even more speed. While, at their rear, the young policeman, who had been lagging behind, had not been able to keep up and was now nowhere in sight. They had lost him!

After curving round a clump of trees, to one side of the grassy area, they came upon a group of five gardeners working in the park. Or, at least, *one* of them was working! The other four just stood around watching the fifth one, who, single-handed, was hauling a large tree-stump out of the ground!

Edison and Willard were astonished to see this, until they recognized the 'tree-hauler'.

'It's Tub!' Willard exclaimed, referring to their friend, the somewhat tubby youth they had met during their first adventure together.

'You mean, it's *Super*-Tub!' Edison corrected. Like Gran, Tub had become Super during their adventure.

So that was why he was doing all the work, while the others stood around watching him.

Super Gran skimmed the vehicle up to them, stopped it and opened the dome.

'Hello, Tub,' the children greeted him. 'Want to come for a ride?'

'Whew!' Tub pulled the stump right out of the ground, threw it to one side, wiped his brow and then looked towards the Skimmer. 'Oh, hi folks!'

'Wow! That was some yank!' Willard exclaimed admiringly.

'Where's the American?' Edison joked, pretending

to look round. 'Yank — American . . . get it?' She laughed.

But no one else seemed to see the joke!

'Yeah,' one of the workmen agreed, 'it wasn't a bad pull — considering Tub's so fat!'

'I'm not fat — it's muscles!' Tub protested, glaring at the man. Then he turned back again to Super Gran and company. 'What's this?'

'It's a Skimmer,' exclaimed Willard (who was still trying to work out Edison's joke!).

Super Gran glanced nervously behind her. 'Look, Tub, I don't want to rush you, laddie, but we've . . . ah . . . really got to be . . . um . . . on our way. D'you want to come for a wee trip with us, or not?' She didn't want the policeman catching up with them and spoiling their fun.

'Yeah. Sure, sure,' Tub said. 'It's time for me tea-break anyway, isn't it, fellas?' He appealed to the other men, who were producing flasks of hot water, tea-bags, mugs and sandwiches — from nowhere, it seemed — ready for a break. (And, as if by magic, there appeared in Tub's hand a ham sandwich, which he proceeded to munch!)

'Sure, you go ahead, Tub,' one of the men said. 'You've earned your tea-break.'

'*Tea*-break?' Edison giggled. '*Tree*-break is more like it!'

So Tub clambered aboard, the dome was closed and the Skimmer shot off on its travels again, heading in the direction of the boating-lake. And it did so only seconds before a hot, sweating, exhausted, eager young policeman came into sight and approached the gardeners to ask them if they had seen a flying saucer heading that way!

At the lake, Super Gran plunged the Skimmer down the slope at the edge and into the water — hoping that it wouldn't sink! She pressed the switch to start the outboard motor, then waited to see if it would or wouldn't work. It worked, changing the Skimmer from a motor-car into a motor-boat.

She zoomed it around the lake a couple of times, getting the 'feel' of the new controls she'd now have to use and trying, at the same time, *not* to collide with or swamp the other craft on the water, the canoes and rowing-boats.

'This is great, Super Gran!' Edison cried. 'See? I *told* you it would work as a boat, didn't I?'

'And it flies, too!' Willard told Tub, who was sitting beside him in the back seat. 'At least, so *she* says.' He nodded in Edison's direction.

'Does it?' Tub was impressed. 'Try it, Super Gran. Make it fly!'

'Well, *hover* is a better word for it, I believe,' Super Gran told him. 'At least, so Mr Black said. Anyway, I'll have a shot at it. Here goes . . .'

But before Super Gran could find the controls to make the Skimmer fly, Edison had some bad news for her.

'Oh-oh, Super Gran — over there . . .!' She pointed.

'Not the policeman?'

'No. On the landing-stage. The boatman. He's shaking his fist at us.'

'Oh no,' Super Gran groaned, distracted from the controls. 'Not yon same sour-faced wee character we had all the trouble with the last time?'

The children explained to Tub that the boatman had once tried to stop her rescuing a small girl from drowning in the lake – and had accused Super Gran of only being in the water for a swim!

The boatman, standing red-faced on the landing-stage, pulled a battered old whistle from his pocket and blew it at them. Which, of course, made him even *more* red-faced!

'Hey! You lot! Stop! Come here! You can't use unauthorized, non-town-council water-craft on my boating-lake! And you haven't paid, either! Get off my lake!'

'*His* lake?' Edison muttered. 'Humph! The cheek of him! It isn't *his* lake – it's the town council's lake. It's *every*one's lake!'

'Just ignore him, Gran,' Willard advised.

The boatman turned to a small boy who was waiting at the head of the queue with his older sister for a boat.

'Here, sonny, go and fetch me one of the Park Rangers, will you?'

'Huh?' The boy looked at him, blankly. 'Queen's Park Rangers?'

'Not *Queen's* Park Rangers – one of the *Park* Rangers!' He saw that he wasn't getting anywhere with the boy, so he turned to his sister: 'Here, girlie, *you* go and fetch one, will you?'

'An' lose me place in the queue? You're not on!' She scowled at him darkly.

'I promise you won't lose your place. I just want you to fetch . . .'

'Hey mister, there's a cop — will *he* do?' The small boy tugged at the boatman's jacket sleeve, and pointed.

'A cop . . . er . . . a policeman? The very thing. Great!'

He took a closer look at the rapidly approaching constable, and recognized him. 'Why, it's my young nephew, Rupert — that's even better. A keen young lad, is Rupert. Keen to get promotion, keen to get on in the force. *He*'ll soon sort that lot out, he will!'

If Super Gran and company had heard this they would have realized why the policeman looked so sour-faced — he was related to the boatman, and sour faces obviously ran in that family!

The policeman reached the landing-stage and blew his whistle at the Skimmer. And shook his fist. And jumped up and down.

'We'd better go over, Super Gran,' Edison said, worriedly.

'Aye, lassie, I suppose we'd better.' She guided the Skimmer to the landing-stage, but left its engine running.

'Can I see your driving licence?' the constable asked, when Super Gran had raised the dome.

'Don't have one!' she confessed.

'Ah! Then let me see your M.O.T. certificate,' he demanded.

'Don't have one of those, either!'

'Insurance certificate?'

'Nope!'

'A licence to use this . . . this . . . vehicle on the boating-lake?'

'Nope!'

'Ah!' The constable grinned. *Now* they were for it. He'd have the old lady on about twenty different charges — at least! And he'd get promotion in no time. He beamed. 'Well, I'm going to have to arrest you *and* your vehicle, and . . .'

Super Gran, reading the man's mind and discovering all the charges he was going to bring against her, waited to hear no more!

4 'Air' We Go Again!

'Oh, and I haven't got a pilot's licence, either!' Super
Gran beamed, as she slammed the dome down, put the
Skimmer into gear and zoomed it away from the
landing-stage; away from the flabbergasted policeman
and his uncle, the boatman, who could only stand
there staring, puzzled.

'Pilot's licence? What's she talking about?' Rupert
asked.

'*I* dunno,' his sour-faced boatman uncle shrugged.
'And where are they off to?' The Skimmer had
disappeared behind the island in the centre of the lake.
'What're they up to?'

'*I* dunno either,' Rupert admitted.

'Well, young Rupert, lad, *do* something about it.
Don't just stand there.'

'What'll I do, Uncle Herbert?'

'*I* don't know. *You're* the policeman. You're supposed
to know about these things, not me.'

The only thing they could think of to do was to
jump into a rowing-boat and row out to the island
after the Skimmer.

'And what was that she said about a pilot's licence,
Uncle?' Rupert asked again, as they rowed.

'*I* don't know,' the boatman replied.

They soon found out!

Super Gran had decided to try out the Skimmer as an aircraft. She revved up the engine and then, after checking its 'flight' controls, she pulled a lever. The retractable wings at the side unfolded.

'Well, folks – here goes!' she said. 'Keep your fingers crossed that it works. And you'd better keep your toes and your eyes crossed as well!'

They were on their way. It was now or never!

'Are . . . are you sure you should, Super Gran?' Edison asked, having second thoughts about the whole thing.

The Skimmer came round the corner from behind the island, back into the view of the two men, who were chasing it in the rowing-boat.

'Hey! What's that noise?' the boatman asked, looking round as he rowed – and adding 'Yeeks!' at what he saw approaching them.

'What *is* it?' Rupert also looked round – to see the Skimmer bearing down on them at speed, its wings extended for flight.

Both of them – as one man! – stood up in the rowing-boat as the Skimmer came nearer. They shook their fists at it as it passed them only a few metres away. The boat swayed in the Skimmer's waves. The men lost their balance and fell overboard into the shallow – but extremely muddy – weedy water.

'Oh-oh!' Super Gran, meanwhile, was saying at the controls, 'we haven't got up enough speed yet to fly . . .!'

'What'll we do, Gran?' Willard asked.

'We'll have to do another circuit of the loch,' she

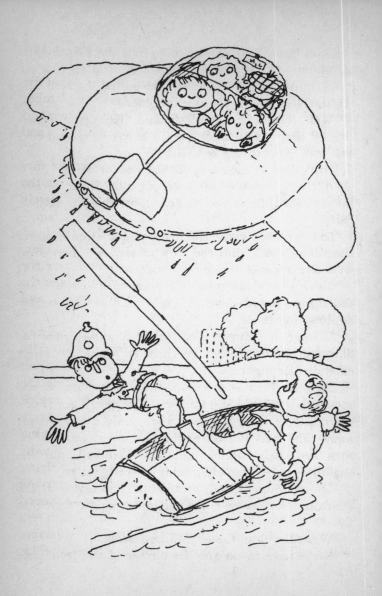

said grimly. 'That'll give us a better run at it and increase our speed. I hope!'

So while the Skimmer disappeared round behind the island again, the two men took the chance to clamber out of the water and into their boat. But no sooner had they got back in than the Skimmer reappeared – and this time heading straight for them!

They stood in the boat again and shook their fists again – but this time they had to duck down as the Skimmer, in lifting off the surface of the lake, barely cleared their heads! They toppled overboard again – their hands still upraised in a fist-shaking gesture!

The Skimmer continued on its way, gaining height, over the boat-hut on the landing-stage and over the cheering, yelling, waving, queueing children; over the trees, rose gardens, play-park areas, tennis courts, and out towards the park's perimeter fence.

It took Super Gran only a few minutes of flying around inside the park to get the hang of the aircraft's controls, then she made it swoop, dive, bank and climb all over the place. After that she flew it outside the park and terrorized not only Edison but also everyone she flew over!

One woman, in a near-by garden hanging out her washing, dropped it with fright into a muddy puddle at the sight of what she thought was a UFO, flying just above her house! Another housewife was carrying home a bag of groceries when the Skimmer swooped low over her, causing her to drop – and smash – a dozen eggs! A joiner, working on the roof of a garage, looked up, saw the Skimmer, took his attention off his descending hammer — and hammered his fingers! And a herd of cows in a field which they flew over took one look at the skimming, zooming Skimmer — and stampeded!

'Everyone thinks this is a flying saucer,' Edison said. 'A UFO.'

'It *is* a UFO,' Super Gran grinned, 'it's an Unforgettable Flying Oldie!'

'Hey!' Tub suddenly remembered, 'me tea-break'll be over! You'd better take me back!'

So that was the end of the test-flight, as Super Gran landed the Skimmer in the park again, dropping Tub off near his astonished workmates. Then, after retracting the wings and converting the vehicle into a 'car' again, she skimmed it across the grass, through the park, to the exit nearest Mr Decker's factory.

'I think we'll take the Skimmer up to London when we go,' Super Gran suggested.

'London? Who's goin' to London?' Willard asked, his eyes gleaming. This was the first that he had heard of Super Gran's trip.

She explained, as she drove, all about the exhibition and that he and Edison could go with her, repeating that she thought they should take the Skimmer with them. But Edison was horrified at the idea!

'You can't take it there!' she said. 'If it careers about the way it did today — it'll bring the whole of London to a standstill!'

'Och! Blethers, lassie!' Super Gran argued, dismissing the girl's fears. 'That was only while I got the hang of it. Don't panic!'

But Edison wasn't going to be convinced as easily as that — as Super Gran later discovered.

'Is Tub coming to London with us?' Willard asked.

Super Gran shook her head. 'I don't suppose he'll get time off his work.'

They reached the factory yard and climbed out of the vehicle, leaving it with its proud inventor and its equally proud builder. After giving a report on their test-'skim' and test-flight to Mr Black, Super Gran had a few quiet words with Mr Decker, who she knew was an important businessman.

'Oh . . . ah . . . Mr Decker, sir . . . I've got a wee job for you to do . . .'

'Yes, Super Gran? What's that?' he beamed.

'I want you to speak to the police about me . . .'

'The police . . .?'

'Something tells me they'll be charging me . . .'

'Charging you,' he interrupted, 'how much?' He guffawed heartily.

'Charging me,' Super Gran continued, 'with-driving dangerously, skimming dangerously, motor-boating dangerously and flying dangerously!'

'Oh . . .!' That took the smile off the man's face!

'Driving without road tax, insurance, M.O.T. certificate and number plates . . .'

'Oh-oh . . .!'

'Resisting arrest, disturbing the peace . . .'

'Uh?' This was the first time they had seen Mr Decker without his eternal jovial grin. 'And how do you think *I* am going to talk them out of *that* lot?' he asked.

43

'Och, that'll be nae bother at a' to you,' Super Gran flattered him. 'Besides, it was you — and your friend there — who let us take the Skimmer out without all yon documents, so there! And you can also tell them that I'm Super Gran — the one who foiled yon bank-raid for them, and put yon Inventor's baddies to flight.' She smiled broadly. 'See what you can do, eh?'

On the Monday of the following week Super Gran, Edison and Willard went up to London for the 'Modern Times' exhibition — on a lorry!

Edison didn't think that that was the best way to travel. It wasn't the most comfortable way, and it wasn't the most elegant way for a would-be celebrity (Super Gran) to travel. But Mr Silver, the exhibition organizer, had had to hire the lorry to transport the Skimmer and their luggage. And, as they didn't want to let the vehicle out of their sight, in case it was stolen, they'd had no option but to travel with it.

Even to get the Skimmer *this* far had been an achievement for Super Gran. For she'd had to argue strongly with Edison to convince her that they should take it. Much as the girl had enjoyed jaunting about in it, she still felt that it was too dangerous to take to London.

'If we don't take the Skimmer, I won't take you to the zoo, lassie,' Super Gran had threatened, knowing that Edison had been keen to visit Regent's Park Zoo while in London.

'Oh well, that's that, then. If I can't go, I can't go!' Edison was disappointed — but determined! 'Look at the panic it caused here in Chisleton, never mind London!'

But Super Gran appealed to the girl's pride in her father and his inventions. She knew that Edison wanted him to become famous.

'With all those reporters and television people and cameras he'll be famous overnight, once his Skimmer is seen on the telly. It'll bring him fame and fortune.'

'We-ell . . .' Edison was dithering. 'Maybe you're right . . .'

' 'Course I'm right. Amn't I *al*ways right? Amn't I Super Gran?'

So Edison, reluctantly, was persuaded. Although, just to have the last word, she couldn't resist having a go at the way Super Gran spoke. '*Aren't* I, Super Gran.'

'Aren't you what, lassie?'

'No. I mean, "*aren't* I", not "*amn't* I",' she explained.

'*Amn't* I? Oh — that's the way we Scots say it,' Super Gran said.

'Oh, I see. And how do *big* Scots say it?' Edison joked.

Mr Silver had decided that he had better get police permission before letting the Skimmer loose in London. (And even then it was doubtful, they told him, if it would be allowed on public highways. It would probably have to be used only on and over London's public parks, commons and heaths.)

'Where are we takin' the Skimmer, Gran?' Willard asked, as the lorry entered the suburbs of London.

'Mr Silver arranged for it to be stored safely at a warehouse. Let's see now . . .' She pulled a crumpled piece of paper out of her handbag, straightened it out and read the address off it. 'It's a place called "Poley's Warehouse".' She handed the paper to the driver, who glanced briefly at it.

'Oh yeah. I know the place,' he replied, 'it's down near the river. The Thames. No problem.'

But the driver was wrong, there *was* a problem. And the problem was the warehouse's owner, Mr Poley. For Mr Poley was a crook — and Mr Poley had a gang!

'Mr Poley?' Super Gran asked the completely bald, fat, round little man who greeted them at the opened double doors of the warehouse. 'I'm Super Gran.'

The man had a short, fat neck and short, fat arms and legs. He looked like a tennis ball balanced precariously on top of a huge beer-barrel — with legs! — and he gave the impression that if he were to fall over he would roll away!

An instant nickname for the man jumped into Super Gran's mind: 'Roly Poley'! And, although she didn't know it at the time, this was exactly what *everyone*, friend and foe alike, called him. (But not to his face — he was touchy about the name!)

'This is the Skimmer,' Super Gran went on. 'Mr Silver arranged for it to be stored here. He said it would be safe.'

'Worry not, dear lady, I shall endeavour to keep my eye on it,' Roly Poley replied, eyeing it with interest and wondering just what kind of vehicle it was.

He didn't have to wait long to find out!

'It's a car, a boat and a sort of hoverin' aeroplane!' Willard informed him excitedly.

46

'Ah! M'mm, I see, I see.' Mr Poley's interest grew.

'And *my* Dad invented it,' Edison added proudly, not to be outdone.

Roly rubbed his hands together gleefully. He had just decided that the Skimmer was the very thing to help him get ahead in his career as a crook. It could be the answer to a lot of problems. It would make the ideal getaway car.

And it was going to be his . . .!

5   Roly, the Pole and the Punk

Roly shouted towards a little office at the side of the
warehouse for his two assistants (who were actually his
gang-members) to come and help the lorry driver
unload the Skimmer and bring it into the building.

The first assistant to emerge was promptly christened
the 'Pink Punk' by Super Gran in a whisper to the
children. He was about the oldest punk in London – or
anywhere else! He was about fifty years old (which, to
Willard and Edison, was ancient!) and he was pink
from head to foot! He had pink spiky hair and he wore
a pink suit, festooned with safety pins and zips. Even
his boots and socks were pink! His shirt was pink and
his tie was pink. He was *all* pink!

The man, although as broad as Roly, was taller and
stronger – which helped in lugging about the TV sets,
music centres, hi-fi sets and fridges which Roly and his
gang stole and hi-jacked.

The other gang-member (or 'assistant', as Roly
called him in public!) was as thin as a clothesline! He
was tall, skinny and wiry, and because of his size and
shape was nick-named the 'Beanpole' by his friends,
though this was usually shortened to the 'Pole'.

Roly introduced him as 'one of my assistants, the
Pole', adding, to him, 'Fetch the Skimmer off the lorry
into the warehouse, will you?'

'Okay, boss,' the Pole said, adding, to the Pink Punk, 'Come on, mate . . .'

'Oh,' said Super Gran, 'he speaks good English for a Pole, doesn't he?'

'He is not *that* kind of Pole!' Roly corrected. 'He is the *Bean*pole!'

'Oh?' said Edison, brightly. 'He's *been* a Pole — but he's English now?'

While Roly, with a sigh, explained what he had meant, his two men helped the driver to off-load the Skimmer and wheel it into a corner of the warehouse. Then, as Roly walked around the machine, inspecting it closely, Super Gran jumped up to the cab, stretched inside, locked the anti-theft device and put the key into her handbag.

She and the children then left, to be driven to their hotel — where a few eyebrows shot up when they arrived aboard a rather old lorry!

'Wow! What a posh place!' Willard cried in admiration.

'Look, Super Gran!' Edison exclaimed when they saw their suite of rooms. 'We've even got our own bathroom and radio and telephone and colour telly and tea-maker and digital alarm clock!'

'And just look at that fancy food,' Super Gran said — later — when they sat down to lunch in the dining-room and looked at the menu.

Meanwhile, Roly was gloating over the Skimmer, which he now reckoned was as good as his!

Roly was, in a small way, a businessman; and, also in a small way, he was a crook.

The warehouse he ran, from which he supplied shops and department stores with foodstuffs and furniture, was mainly just a 'front' for his criminal activities. He was on his way up in the world. That is, in the *under*world! He and his gang of two had been involved, until now, in hi-jacking lorry-loads of goods which they brought to the warehouse, and which were then passed on to the public, undetected, along with the genuine goods.

Now he was secretly planning a 'big job'. One which would not only bring a fortune but would also make his fellow-crooks look on him as an equal — instead of a blunderer! For the truth was that so far Roly hadn't been very successful.

It was not so much that Roly himself was a blunderer, it was more that his gang were blunderers. For they *would* insist on hi-jacking loads which were not easily marketed among the ordinary goods which Roly sold — loads like: a tanker full of milk! A load of waste paper! A consignment of 70,000 nuts, bolts, screws and washers!

As well as that, the Pink Punk also tended to blunder in a personal way. He kept forgetting that his style of dress was so distinctive as to be a dead give-away when he was out on a job. After all, even the worst eye-witness to a crime was not likely to over-look a criminal who dressed like a middle-aged punk, all in pink!

'You will have to wear a raincoat, to hide your pink

suit,' Roly had told him on one occasion. 'And a stocking mask.' (To hide his spiky pink punk hair.)

And he did. Only, the raincoat had been a plastic, transparent one! And, because he was so proud of his hair, the mask covered his face all right — but he'd cut the top off it, to show off his fancy hairstyle!

However, all thoughts of his incompetent gang went swiftly out of Roly's mind when he discovered that he had a problem with the Skimmer — the anti-theft device, which he hadn't noticed Super Gran locking.

'I saw the old crow putting a key into her bag,' the Pole said.

'Then we shall have to get it away from her,' Roly declared, after they had all had a go at the lock and had found that it was most definitely un-pickable. 'Now, which hotel is she staying at?'

'Dunno,' his men replied, with blank expressions.

As none of them knew anything about Super Gran's arrangements, Roly had to phone Mr Silver to find out.

'Ah, and she is doing a demonstration at the "Modern Times" exhibition at King's Court, is she?' Roly said into the phone after the man had given him the name of Super Gran's hotel. 'I see, I see.'

'An exhibition? What kinda exhibition, boss?' the Punk asked him, as he ran a steel comb through his greasy pink hair.

Roly, putting the phone down, shrugged, the fat on his neck wobbling dangerously. 'What does *any* little old lady demonstrate at an exhibition? Knitting, crocheting, baking a cake, making home-made jam? Who knows?'

If the Pole and the Punk had known just *what* Super Gran was there to demonstrate, they might not have been so keen to comply with their employer's instructions when he told them to go and find her. No, they didn't know just then — they found out later!

While the Punk left the warehouse to go and steal a getaway car, Roly instructed the Pole:

'Remember, we do not want her to know what we are up to. Especially me. *I* am supposed to be an honest businessman, not a crook.'

'Sure, boss.'

'So I want you to *sneak* the key away from the old bat . . . er . . . lady. Pick her pocket. Snatch her handbag. Whatever.'

'Sure boss, sure. No problem,' the Pole assured him.

At the hotel, the two men parked the stolen car and entered the plush foyer.

'We're looking for that there Super Gran,' the Pole told the man at the reception desk.

'Who?' The receptionist leafed through his register, after staring disgustedly, and sniffing loudly, at the men. 'We do not seem to have anyone of *that* name staying here,' he insisted snootily, slamming the register shut with a loud, final bang.

'Oh, *you* know,' the Pole said, 'a li'l old lady and a coupla kids . . .?'

The man tended to look down his long, thin nose at *all* the hotel's guests, and especially at Super Gran and the children, who were that bit lower down the social scale than the others. But he looked even further down his nose at these two specimens — who were at the *bottom* of the social scale!

'Ah, you mean Mrs Smith and party?' he said, the light dawning. 'Whom shall I say is calling?' He reached towards his telephone.

'Well this,' said the Punk, pointing to his mate, 'is the Pole, and I'm . . .'

'Pole? Oh, I say, he speaks very good . . . ah-um . . . English, for a Polish . . . ah . . . gentleman,' the receptionist smiled, condescendingly.

'He ain't that kinda Pole,' the Punk explained, 'he's the *Bean*pole.'

'Oh, he's *been* a Pole . . .?'

'Never mind all *that*, mate,' the Punk scowled. 'Now, about that there li'l old lady . . .' He glowered at the man from close range, a (bloodshot) eyeball-to-eyeball confrontation, and the receptionist gulped. 'Wot's 'er room number?'

The man gulped again, and gave in! 'Oh . . . ah . . . um . . .' He hurriedly opened his register again and thumbed through its pages. 'Mrs Smith . . . let me see . . . suite number 304.' He turned to the telephone again. 'I shall just call up and see if she is in . . .'

He looked up — but the men were gone. They had shot across the foyer and were already inside the lift, the doors of which were closing.

'Here, I say . . .' the receptionist exclaimed, realizing that he had allowed two obnoxious, disreputable characters to run about loose in his posh hotel. What would the manager say? He quaked at the thought.

Roly's men arrived at the door of Super Gran's suite,

but by then the Pole had completely forgotten his boss's instructions about sneaking the key away from her stealthily.

They knocked on the door. Super Gran opened it. They pushed her aside and barged into the room. 'Give's the key!' demanded the Pole.

'Here! What's the idea, forcing your way in on a poor, unprotected little old lady?' she gasped.

'Never mind the speech, lady, just give us the key. Let's have it,' the Punk said, pushing her roughly into an armchair.

'Here, you wee bachles, we'll have less of that! I'll let you have it, all right!' she protested, as the children stood back, waiting for some action from her.

'Give 'em one, Gran!' Willard urged.

'I will, in a minute, if they don't stop behaving like a couple of wee scunners . . .!'

'Aw, shaddup, you old crow!' the Punk yelled at her. 'That's enough talkin'. Don't waste our time, just hand over . . .'

'I won't waste your *time*,' Super Gran interrupted, her temper up, as she bounced nimbly out of her chair towards the astonished crooks, 'I'll waste your *faces*!'

She leapt forward and her little old fists shot out, each one connecting with the stomach of each crook.

'Ouch!' they gasped in surprise — and pain!

'I'm warning you . . .' Super Gran began.

'And *I'm* warning *you*,' the Punk gulped when he'd got his breath back, pointing, with the hand which wasn't clutching his sore solar plexus, at the Pole, 'he's got a black belt, in karate . . .'

54

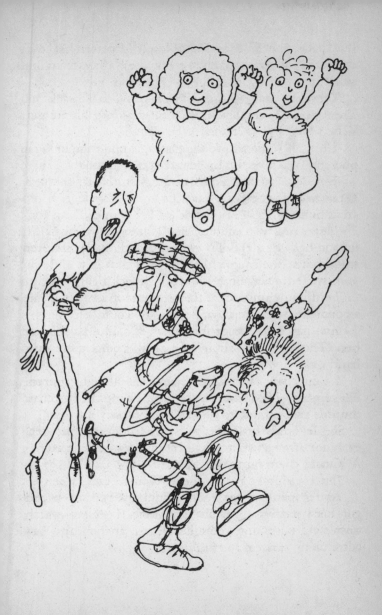

'Yeah,' the Pole muttered, taking his hands away from his suffering stomach to take up a karate stance, arms at the ready. 'Yeah, one chop from me, and . . .'

'Humph!' snorted Super Gran. 'The only black belt about *him* — is the one *about* him! Holding his trousers up!'

'Eh?' Both men took their attention off Super Gran and the Pole dropped his karate stance, as each of them looked down at the Pole's trousers to see if, as Super Gran said, his belt *was* black!

While their attention was off her, Super Gran took the opportunity to launch herself into a flying dropkick, as she had seen the TV wrestlers doing on Saturday afternoons! She caught the Punk on the chest and sent him sprawling against the door, knocking the breath from him again. And then, before the Pole could appreciate what was happening or could recover his karate stance, she went into a karate stance herself and proceeded to karate-chop the man about his arms, sides and back.

'*I'll* give you carrots and chops!' she fumed — and the Pole, aching, fled from the room, hauling the battered, bruised and bewildered Punk behind him.

Super Gran couldn't resist running out into the corridor after them to give them a few more thumps — to help them on their way!

'That was Roly Poley's men,' Willard said, when his Gran returned to the room and they had all settled down to recover from the invasion. 'They were after the key for the anti-theft device. So that means they were tryin' to steal the Skimmer!'

56

'You'd better phone Mr Poley, Super Gran,' Edison suggested, 'and tell him that his assistants are baddies. And warn him to watch out for them. And to guard the Skimmer. And maybe they'll steal from *him*, too.'

'Good idea, lassie, I'll do that.' And she went to leave the room again.

'Where are you going, Super Gran?' Edison smiled, pointing to the telephone which stood on the writing-desk in a corner of the room. 'You've got a phone right here! Remember? You don't have to go downstairs for it!'

'Och aye, I keep forgetting that this is a posh hotel!' Super Gran laughed. 'I can't get used to having a room with its own telephone and colour telly and everything.' She sat down at the desk, lifted the phone and asked to be put through to Poley's warehouse.

You look a bit tired, Super Gran, Edison thought, as she watched the old lady sitting at the desk, phoning. Maybe the fight was too much for her?

'What is that, Super Gran?' Roly was saying on the phone, pretending to be shocked by the news. 'My assistants are crooks? No! Surely not! Do not tell me that! Oh, that *is* awful. Terrible! Yes, I certainly shall look out for them *and* for the Skimmer. You may rest assured, dear lady, that I shall not take my eyes *off* the Skimmer from now on.' And Roly really meant what he said, but not in the way Super Gran thought he did!

How on earth, he wondered, when he put the phone down, had his men bungled *this* job? All they had had to do was quietly snatch a little old key away from a little old lady. And they had botched it up, the bally blunderers! They were hopeless!

They were also sore when they arrived back at the warehouse to relate how a seemingly harmless, weak, little old lady had foiled two big, strong, tough baddies — by herself!

But Roly wasn't really surprised. For when the men entered his office they found him watching the news on a new portable TV set. (That is, a newly stolen TV set!) He pointed to a short item concerning the opening of the 'Modern Times' exhibition, showing Super Gran performing some of her Super-stunts: Super-strength, Super-hearing, Super-eyesight, X-ray eyesight! Roly gasped and turned to his bruised and battered boys: 'First thing tomorrow go along to that exhibition and find out just what powers she has got. While I think of a way to get that key away from her . . .'

6   Mr Fry from Department Y

'Cor! Look at that!' the Pink Punk exclaimed, from the back of the crowd who were watching Super Gran going through her paces at the 'Modern Times' exhibition.

He and the Pole had paid their entrance money and had made their way past the 'Modern House' stand, the 'Ideal Car', the 'Super Yachts' and the 'Supa-Dupa Hi-Fi' stands, to get to the far end of the exhibition hall where Super Gran was performing, surrounded by a throng of people – who could hardly believe their eyes!

First of all the old lady did a spot of weight-lifting – by hoisting a Super-heavyweight weightlifter into the air! Then she Super-sprinted along the inside length of the building, racing (and beating!) a very embarrassed Olympic athlete – who had suddenly started to limp, just after Super Gran passed him, as an excuse for being beaten! And after that she demonstrated her Super-eyesight by reading the small print on a notice – at the farthest end of the building! Then she Super-heard one of the attendants, who had been positioned about three hundred metres away, and thought-read another one. Then, to round off her performance, she Super-jumped over a caravan – and then towed it behind her, at a fast trot, from one end of the building to the other!

'Cor!' the Punk repeated, impressed, at the end of her stint. 'So that's wot we was up against yesterday. Wow!'

'Yeah,' said the Pole, 'and the next time we tackle her we'd best take six of the lads with us!'

Meanwhile, the Skimmer had come to the attention of a government department! Application for permission to drive it and fly it around London had been passed from the police to a certain office called Department Y. And Mr Silver, at the exhibition, had a phone call from them which was, to say the least, somewhat confusing!

'This is Department Y,' a spokesman informed him.

'Y?' said Mr Silver.

'Just because that's what it's called, old boy,' the civil servant told him.

'Yes, but why Y?' Mr Silver asked, getting caught up in asking a question he hadn't wanted to ask!

'No, old boy,' the spokesman corrected, 'not YY – just Y, etcetera.'

'I didn't mean that,' Mr Silver went on, 'I meant – *why* is Department Y phoning me?'

'It's about this vehicle, the . . . Slimmer, is it?'

'The Skimmer,' Mr Silver corrected. 'But I was dealing with the local police office about it.'

'Ah! But from what we've heard, etcetera, about this . . . ah . . . um . . . Scanner . . . no, Skinner, is it? No, the . . . ah . . . um . . .?'

'The Skimmer, the Skimmer,' Mr Silver corrected again, patiently.

'Ah, yes, the Slummer. Well anyway, from what

we've heard of this Stammer, it is an extremely versatile
— even an extraordinarily versatile — vehicle . . .!'

'It certainly seems to be,' Mr Silver agreed.

'And it is therefore too special, etcetera,' the Department Y man went on, 'to be used — or to be *owned*, for that matter — by just anyone, etcetera. Oh dear me, no. Or yes. As the case may be, etcetera.'

'Huh? Pardon?' Mr Silver was more confused than ever.

'In other words, old boy, it must — it simply *must* — be handed over, straight away, to the army . . .!'

'The army?'

'The army. For them to inspect. To test its capabilities. To prevent its falling into enemy hands, etcetera.'

'But . . . but surely there's no need . . .?' Mr Silver began.

'Afraid so, old boy,' the spokesman said, cutting him short. 'We're sending one of our chief operatives, a Mr Fry, to inspect the machine at that warehouse where you're holding it, etcetera.'

'Mr Fry?'

'No, *I'm* not Mr Fry. *He's* Mr Fry. Mr Fry from Department Y. He's on his way now, etcetera. Cheerypip!'

Feeling as if he had just been through a spin-dryer, Mr Silver put the phone down. He was utterly confused. The government? The army? Mr Fry from Department Y? Etcetera?

It was all too much for Mr Silver, who had plenty of other problems connected with the exhibition to worry about. But at least this was a problem which he could get rid of! He phoned Roly Poley at the warehouse – to 'pass the buck' to him!

'The government? The army? Mr Fry from Department Y?' said Roly, echoing Mr Silver's own thoughts.

'*I* don't know why,' Mr Silver snapped. 'I'm just passing . . . oh, I see what you mean. Yes, Department Y, that's right. All very secret and hush-hush – etcetera!' (Even *he* was saying it now!) 'But I'm sure I can leave it in your hands, eh? I can trust *you*.'

Then you *are* a fool, if you trust *me*! Roly thought, chuckling quietly to himself.

'You'll look out for Mr Fry, then?'

'I certainly will,' Roly told him, resolving to do something about the Skimmer before Mr Fry arrived to take charge of it and put it out of his reach.

However, he was too late! For no sooner had Roly put his phone down than a small man with a rather nervous moustache and a worried-looking face, in a raincoat and bowler hat and carrying a briefcase and a rolled umbrella, arrived at the warehouse.

'Er . . . Mr Poley?' Mr Fry looked nervously round the warehouse until his eye caught the large white bulge which was the tarpaulin-covered Skimmer standing quietly in its corner. 'I'm Mr Fry – from Department Y.' (He said it as if he were saying a poem!)

'Yes . . . ah . . . I was expecting you.' Roly's mind was working overtime. How could he get rid of this little pest without handing the Skimmer over to him? Should he consider bopping him on the bonce with something?

Before he could make any plans, the rather weedy-looking Mr Fry turned and called out over his shoulder to two tall, broad, muscular men, who appeared threateningly in the open doorway behind him. So Roly, being alone and unsupported by his gang, decided not to argue!

Little Mr Fry, followed by his burly henchmen, went over to the Skimmer, lifted a corner of its cover and inspected the machine.

Roly thought quickly. 'The only thing is,' he explained, smiling in triumph as he remembered it, 'the Skimmer cannot be moved until it is unlocked, and I do not have the key.' He grinned. *That* should delay them for a while. It would also delay *him*, of course, but *he* could get someone to break into the lock before the weedy little Mr Fry – that small fry! – could get the key from Super Gran.

'A little old Scottish lady has the key,' he volunteered, 'but I do not know how to contact her. I am sorry.'

This was a lie, of course, and he smiled as he said 'sorry', so Mr Fry suspected that there was something funny going on. But he didn't know what.

'Mr Silver, the exhibition man – I think *he* knows where I can contact her?' Mr Fry said.

'Ah . . . um . . . yes,' Roly replied. 'That is so.'

'May I therefore use your teleph – ?'

'No!' Roly bawled at him, before he finished asking. 'Ah, that is . . . I mean . . . it is not working, I am afraid. So sorry.'

But he smiled again as he apologized and Mr Fry, as he and his men turned away to go in search of a public phone box, was certain that Roly was lying again about the phone. But why? There was definitely something peculiar going on here, he decided as he left.

He phoned Mr Silver, got the address of Super Gran's hotel, and set off to contact her.

A few minutes later, when Roly's gang returned to the warehouse to report — rather fearfully! — on Super Gran's Super-powers, their boss brushed aside their news with *his* news about Mr Fry and *his* men.

'So you see,' Roly concluded, 'we shall have to make another attempt at getting that key away from Super Gran. Either that or we shall have to get one of your friends to break into the lock for us. Because we need the Skimmer more than Super Gran, the government or the army need it. Not to mention Department Y.'

'Y?' said the Pole.

'Why? Because we need it to pull off the "big job", that is why!' Roly snapped.

'No, boss, I meant, Depart — ?'

Roly suddenly had an idea. 'One of you,' he nodded towards the Punk, 'follow Super Gran and those children about, and see if you cannot get a chance to snatch the key from her handbag. While you, Bean-pole, contact your friend "Keys" Stone and get him to make a key for that lock. All right?'

But it wasn't all right with the Punk! 'Hey? Why *me*?' He didn't relish the thought of having to face up to Super Gran again, not on his own, anyway. Not without another six thugs with him! His bruises still pained him. 'Why is it always *me* has to do all the dirty work, eh? Why does *he* get off with it?' He glared at the Pole.

'I shall give you a nice new pair of pink boots if you do it,' Roly offered, knowing that *that* would persuade the man.

'Well, why didn't you say that in the first place, boss?'

Meanwhile, Super Gran and the children were arriving back at their hotel from the exhibition hall, and Super Gran had something nagging at her mind. Something which she couldn't quite put her finger on. A feeling. A feeling which she had felt just after she had given her afternoon performance. A peculiar feeling. A feeling which she hadn't felt for some time now.

She was about to say something about it to the children, when Willard said:

'Hey, Gran, those three men over there have been followin' us!' He pointed to the weedy, nervous little Mr Fry with his two henchmen walking a pace behind him, one at each side of him, protectively.

'Following *us*?' Super Gran said. 'What? That worried-looking wee man?'

'Oh no,' gasped Edison, 'not *another* lot! Oh Super Gran, what are *they* after, do you think?'

Super Gran and company had reached the hotel steps, had climbed them, and were now turning round to see the men, who were advancing towards them. Mr Fry put his hand up to stop them and to tell Super Gran that he wanted to speak to her.

'They've been followin' us for a while,' Willard whispered. 'I saw them from the taxi . . .'

'Hoi! Hello there, Super Gran,' Mr Fry interrupted. 'Wait a minute . . .'

The mistake his men made was in running forward up the steps, towards Super Gran. If only they had waited until Mr Fry had explained everything. But they didn't! They dashed ahead of their boss, and Super Gran took it as an attack — and swung into action!

She didn't stop to read their minds, or she would have realized that they were government men, and were 'goodies', not 'baddies'. Seeing them attack (she thought!), she took them to be more of Roly's crooked 'assistants'.

Proud of the success she'd had with the flying dropkick against the Pink Punk, she tried it out again! On the first man, as he climbed the hotel steps. And then, as he staggered backwards, she landed on her hands, pushed herself back on to her feet again and let fly with an uppercut to the second man, which landed dead on target.

The first man fell backwards down the steps, collided with little Mr Fry and flattened him, while Super Gran followed up, to the second man, with a left and a right to his jaw and stomach.

'Quick, lassie,' she called over her shoulder to Edison, 'into the hotel. Phone the police. Quick! I'll hold them off. Hurry!'

'No! Stop! Listen!' mumbled a muffled Mr Fry, from under his heavy henchman. 'You don't understand — Y!'

'I *know* I don't understand why!' Super Gran retorted.

'But I'm trying to tell you – Y!' Mr Fry insisted.

'You're not trying to tell me why!' she snapped. 'That's what I want to *know*! Why? What's the big idea? What's this all about?'

She went charging down the steps towards the three men, her arms flailing like demented windmill vanes. But none of them waited until she reached them. They'd had enough!

The two burly bodyguards were offering no further violence towards Super Gran. After all, they were not in the habit of fighting with little old ladies; they wouldn't normally dream of lifting a finger against a little old lady – even in self-defence! And they didn't quite know how to deal with the situation. So they decided not to stand around waiting for her deadly Super-punches to land on them. They ran!

And Mr Fry, having struggled manfully to his feet and decided that it would be better – and safer! – to telephone the old lady and explain, scampered away along the pavement behind his men. He beat a hasty retreat clutching his battered bowler, his bruised briefcase and his broken brolly to his chest, his nervous moustache trembling even more nervously than ever.

'There . . . there must be easier ways,' he told himself as he ran, 'of earning a living . . . !'

7　A Not-So-Super Gran!

'Don't bother, lassie,' Super Gran told a concerned-looking Edison, who stood waiting patiently while the receptionist tried to phone the police. 'Don't bother, son,' she assured the haughty hotel man, who winced at being called 'son'. '*I* cleared them up *without* the police. It's okay.'

'Are you all right, Super Gran?' Edison asked.

'She sure is!' grinned Willard. 'She gave one a dropkick and the other one an uppercut . . .' He demonstrated, against an invisible foe, how she had done it.

'Are you *sure* you're all right?' Edison asked again, seeing Super Gran lowering herself into one of the large basket chairs which posh hotels seem to like to have in their foyers.

''Course I am, lassie,' she said with bravado. But she had to admit to herself that she was just a wee bit tired after her exertion.

After resting for five minutes, she decided that she would go up to their suite.

'Yes, let's go upstairs and get ready for dinner,' said Edison, who thought that Super Gran looked really tired, and could possibly do with a long rest, not just five minutes.

'Right then,' Super Gran said cheerily, after she had

collected the key to the suite from the reception desk, 'I'll race you up the three flights . . . !' She hurried to the foot of the stairs.

'Super Gran!' Edison was shocked. 'Don't be silly! You'll overdo it. You're tired. You're . . .'

'Blethers, lassie! If you two are just a couple of weaklings — then you can take the lift . . . and I'll *still* beat you to it! So there!'

And before either of the children could do a thing about it (and before Willard could race her up the stairs, as he meant to do), Super Gran had sped up them, leaping them three at a time!

Edison and Willard took the lift up to the third floor and walked along the corridor towards their suite, to find the door still shut and the telephone ringing inside. (It was Mr Fry — trying to contact Super Gran the safe way!)

'Where's she got to?' Willard asked, looking up and down the empty corridor.

'She can't be inside, or she'd answer the phone,' Edison pointed out, then her hand shot to her mouth in terror. 'Maybe she's been attacked again, on the way up the stairs!'

'Come on!' Willard ran back along the corridor, towards the lift and the top of the stairs. 'Let's see . . .'

'Wait for me . . .' Edison hurried along in his wake.

They found Super Gran sitting on the top step, safe — but having another rest!

'You okay, Gran?' Willard dropped down to sit beside her.

'Eh? Oh . . . hello. Aye . . . aye, I'm all right, Willie. All right.' She sighed, then smiled wanly.

'Super Gran! *There* you are! Are you all right?' Edison, too, dropped down beside her on the step. 'What happened? You weren't attacked again, were you?'

Super Gran smiled. 'No, no it was nothing like that. I just . . . just felt . . .' She looked puzzled. 'Felt . . . tired . . . !'

'Well, no *wonder* you felt tired,' Edison said, 'you've just been fighting three men, and . . .'

'Aye, but I've fought three men before,' Super Gran argued. 'I've fought *more* than three men before. Yon scunner Inventor and his gang of Toughies,' she reminded them. 'No, it's not that. I had this funny feeling after my demonstrations today. Couldn't think what it was. Hadn't felt it for ages, not since I'd become Super. But I've just realized what it is – I'm tired!' It was unthinkable!

'Well, of *course* you're tired,' Edison agreed. 'You've been performing all your Super-stunts, and . . .'

'Aye, but don't you *see*, lassie?' Super Gran cut in, 'I'm not *supposed* to feel tired. I'm Super Gran. I can do *any*thing . . . !' She smiled weakly. Just at that moment she didn't feel as if she *could* do anything, as she boasted.

Edison tried to smile encouragingly. Her little old friend thought that she could go on for ever without resting.

Super Gran stood up. 'We'd better go to the room. We're blocking the stairs, if anyone wants past us.'

When they reached the suite the telephone had stopped ringing, and Super Gran flopped down into a large, deep, comfortable armchair. 'Och well, they'll probably phone back,' Super Gran said. 'Don't worry.' She pretended that she wasn't as tired as she had been, but Edison wasn't fooled.

'Can we put the telly on, Gran?' Willard asked eagerly, hovering in front of the set, his hand itching to switch it on.

'Aye, sure, laddie. Go ahead.'

As Willard began watching a film, Super Gran muttered, scolding herself: 'I should've been able to run up those flights of stairs in two seconds flat! I must be getting old or something!'

Edison heard this (over the noise of a frantic car-chase through London's crowded streets, on the television) but she had thoughts of her own. Was Super Gran losing her powers, she wondered? For she had noticed that after the old lady's fight with the Pole and the Punk she had sat down to use the phone, and had looked tired then too. And *now* it was the same again. What was happening to her? Was she losing her powers somehow?

'Hey! Look at that!' Willard pointed excitedly at the TV screen, where a car full of crooks, being chased by the police, was in the process of leaping across Tower Bridge while the bridge was opening. And the car at that moment was flying through the air from one part of the bridge, across the gap, to the other. 'Wow!' said the otherwise speechless Willard, as he held his breath until the car cleared the widening gap and landed on the far side, running down the slope to crash through the closed traffic barrier. 'Wow! Did you see that!' He turned to Super Gran. 'Wow! *You* should try that sometime, Gran! I bet you that *you* could do it!'

"*Course* I could,' she smiled. But it was a watery smile, and her heart wasn't in it. Secretly she was wondering if she could jump *any* distance now. There had been a time (until five minutes ago!) when there would have been no question about it.

But wasn't she Super Gran? Couldn't she do *any*-thing? She was beginning to have doubts about *that* now!

Willard kept on and on about the car-jump, and about how Super Gran could easily do it too. But Edison, like Super Gran, was quite sure that somehow, for whatever reason, the old lady was definitely losing her Super-powers . . . !

The next day Mr Fry phoned again, but Super Gran and the children had left the hotel to go to the exhibition, so he missed them again.

After she had finished the day's last performance, Super Gran was rather relieved when a group of press people — reporters and photographers — decided to crowd round to interview and photograph her. For it gave her a much-needed breather. And she was tired. Again. Although she wouldn't admit it to anyone. For people who are Super (and there aren't too many of them around!) aren't supposed to get tired after a few wee stunts, she told herself.

'And to what do you attribute your fantastic powers, Super Gran?' a reporter asked her.

'Well, you see, it was this Super-ray . . .'

'Have you always been Super?' another one interrupted, before she had finished answering the first.

'No, it happened just a wee while ago . . .'

As the cameras clicked and the photographers' lights flashed away, she was interrupted by yet another newspaperman's questions:

'Do you eat any special food? Steaks? Honey? Salads . . . ?'

'No, laddie,' she laughed, 'just porridge . . . !'

'Porridge? *Just* porridge? Nothing but porridge?' The reporter made a face. *Another* porridge-hater! 'Surely not?'

She laughed again. 'No, of course not. Not *just* porridge. Haggis as well! And bannocks, and stovies and . . . !'

'What?'

'No, I'm joking,' she smiled. 'But I eat mainly plain fare, nothing fancy. And I *do* take porridge every morning for breakfast. Couldn't do without it!'

'You said something about a ray . . . ?' another reporter asked, obviously bored by the subject of Super Gran's diet.

After some time, Super Gran and the children managed to escape the press and their rapid-fire questions and made their way out of the exhibition, heading for Regent's Park Zoo, where Super Gran had promised to take Edison.

However, after being there only a little while, and

having seen only a few of the animals, Willard spotted a vision in pink, peeking out at them, from amongst a crowd of people!

'Look!' he pointed, 'it's the Pink . . . !'

'Panther?' asked Edison.

'No, Punk!'

'The Pink Punk?' Super Gran cried. 'That punky-monkey? What's *he* doing here?'

'Looks like he's spyin' on us, Gran!' Willard suggested – correctly, of course, although he didn't know that.

'Well I'm going to find out!' Super Gran decided, frowning. 'I want to know what's going on. What's he after? What are they *all* after? That worried-looking wee man, and everyone! Come on . . . !'

As she gave chase to the man, who threaded his way through the crowd, Super Gran wondered if he was after the Skimmer's key again. She intended catching him – and finding out!

As soon as he realized that he'd been spotted, the Punk stepped behind the people in the crowd, hoping to hide and resume his spying, undetected, later – until he could get a chance to grab her handbag. And the key. But when he saw Super Gran heading his way, he pushed through the throng – and ran!

He wondered, as his pink boots beat out a tattoo on the zoo's concrete pathways, how he had come to be spotted so easily! The thought that it could possibly be his bright pink suit and hair just never entered his pink head!

Large as he was, the Punk was agile and athletic.

Pushing his way past, through and between the various clusters of crowd, and knocking some of them over in the process, he was able to make for the rear of the zoo and Regent's Canal, which runs alongside it. He reached the landing-stage of the water-bus service and, without stopping to think, he leapt aboard one of the water-buses which was just leaving.

'Phew!' he gasped, his chest heaving. 'That was close.'

Meanwhile Super Gran, who played by the rules and *didn't* knock over the people who got in her way, was slowed down by having to dodge around them and reached the landing-stage too late to catch the man.

'Havers!' she muttered, as she saw the Punk's water-bus moving off down the canal. 'He's escaped.'

The others eventually caught up with Super Gran to find her on the landing-stage, waving frantically at them to hurry up and jump aboard the next water-bus, which was filling up, ready to leave. 'Come on!' she urged them. 'We can catch him in this one!'

'But how *can* we?' Edison asked, reasonably. 'He's escaped. And besides, what good will it do, catching him?'

Super Gran sat, thankful for the rest, with the children and the other passengers on seats inside the bus. 'I'll be able to read his mind and find out what's going on. And who that worried-looking wee man is. And what they're all after,' she told them.

The two water-buses, the first one a hundred metres ahead of the second, moved steadily along the canal, past the barges tied up along the banks, until the first one approached the terminus at Little Venice, where the canal opens out into a wide basin. It reached the quay and tied up, and the passengers began disembarking, the Punk pushing his way through the crowd.

Super Gran, on the second water-bus, saw this and jumped to her feet, determined to do something about it.

'But what *can* you do?' Edison frowned. 'We're nowhere near landing. And by the time we do he'll have disappeared into one of those streets round about!' She pointed to the area surrounding the basin.

Super Gran spotted another two water-buses, one sailing *into* and the other sailing *out of* the basin – and she made her move.

'Hey! Where are you goin', Gran?' Willard asked, surprised, as his little old grandmother left them with the other passengers in the cabin – and climbed on to the vessel's roof!

'Super Gran!' Edison cried, shocked. 'You can't do that!'

'No? Just you watch me!' said Super Gran. 'Are you forgetting? I'm Super Gran – and I can do *any*thing . . . !'

8   Canal Capers — Again!

She ran along the roof — being careful not to trip over the life-belts which were attached to it — and she jumped from there on to the roof of the bus which was sailing *into* the basin, ahead of theirs. Landing on this boat and quickly regaining her balance, she ran along its roof and jumped from there on to the roof of the water-bus which was sailing *out* of the basin, away from the quay; and from this one she'd jump on to the Punk's vessel, behind it, and then on to the quay!

'Careful, Super Gran!' Edison shouted after her.

'Cr-rumbs! Look at her go!' Willard gasped. 'Good ol' Gran!'

'I'm   *al*ways . . .   jumping . . .   across . . . canals . . . nowadays,' murmured Super Gran, in mid-leap, in mid-air. 'First . . . for Willie . . . and now . . . after yon . . . Pink Punk!'

Hearing the shouts of the children and the other water-bus passengers and onlookers on the quay, the Punk and his fellow passengers looked round to see what was going on. And saw, and stared open-mouthed at, a little old lady jumping virtually right across a broad canal basin — in a hop-step-and-jump sort of way! While the passengers on the other two water-buses (which Super Gran had been using as stepping-stones!) had been puzzled, wondering what the thumps and the running footsteps were — overhead, on their roofs!

The Punk, seeing the rapidly approaching, leap-frogging Super Gran, should have run off before she reached him on the quay. But he couldn't. He was rooted to the spot — hypnotized by the sight of the little old leaping lady!

'Cor!' one of the watching, open-mouthed quay boatmen muttered. 'Is it leap year, or somefink?'

Super Gran, leaping from the last vessel on to the quay, had only to reach out her hand to catch the Punk, who stood motionless, staring fascinated at her. But something went wrong! For, having done all that successfully, Super Gran spoiled the whole effect on landing by 'doing an Edison'! She tripped over her feet and stumbled helplessly into the waiting crowd!

'Havers!' she cried.

And the crowd, who until that moment had been holding its communal breath in awe of the old lady's feat, suddenly burst out laughing!

The Punk, his 'spell' broken by the tripping, stumbling, crestfallen Super Gran, found that he could move again — and he did! He ran! And Super Gran, on her knees in the middle of the crowd (some of whom were now helping her to her feet), could only watch the splodge of pink in the distance as the Punk leapt off the quay and up on to the roadway, and disappeared round a corner.

Super Gran, realizing that her chase through the zoo and across the water-bus roofs had tired her out, sat down exhausted. And the children, whose water-bus had tied up at the quay, jumped off it and ran over to her.

'What happened, Gran?' Willard asked. 'Did you fall?'

His Gran looked up at him ruefully. 'I suppose I did, Willie. It must be old age, eh?'

'Are you all right, Super Gran?' Edison asked, realizing that she *always* seemed to be asking that question nowadays! She looked so tired too, Edison thought. *Were* her Super-powers leaving her, she wondered? That was about the third time now that something like this had happened. What was causing it? Was it temporary – or permanent? Was this the end of Super Gran?

'No, lassie,' Super Gran muttered grimly, 'it certainly *isn't* the end of Super Gran. So there!'

'Wha . . . what . . .?' Edison was shattered, until she realized that Super Gran had read her mind! Well, at least she still had *that* power!

'Aye, and I've still got my *other* powers as well!' she murmured, reading *that* thought too! 'And I'll prove it to you!'

She bent down, put her hands – palms upwards – flat on the ground and then invited Willard to stand on them.

'What for, Gran?'

'I'm just going to lift you up in the air, that's all,' she explained.

But she wasn't too successful. She managed to lift him a few centimetres off the ground and then, after a lot of puffing and panting, she managed to hoist him one metre into the air. But that was nothing, for Super Gran!

'Och! Scunners!' she muttered. '*Any* little old lady could've done that!' She was angry at herself, and puzzled as to why her powers were waning.

Willard jumped off her hands to the ground, and his Gran sat down once again to rest after all her effort!

'What do you think's wrong, Super Gran?' Edison asked, more concerned than ever.

'Och, it's nothing to worry about, lassie,' she replied, trying to put a 'face' on it. She didn't want to admit that she *was* losing her powers, although it was obvious that she was. She shook her head. 'Something's wrong, all right. But I don't know what it is. Even my performance at the exhibition today wasn't up to my usual standard.' She tried to give them a big encouraging grin. 'Och, don't panic. Whatever it is, it'll pass. You'll see.'

But Edison wondered if it *would* pass. She wondered if she was losing her Super-powers for ever! That would be terrible.

Meanwhile, the Pink Punk, discovering that he wasn't being pursued, had sneaked back to see what was going on. He had seen Super Gran resting, trying to lift Willard, then resting again. And when he sneaked even closer he had overheard the conversation about her loss of Super-powers. So, beaming happily, he tiptoed off to report this information to his boss, Roly Poley.

'What?' Roly exclaimed, when he heard about this. 'That is great news. Well done. This is our chance, now that she has lost her powers, to get the Skimmer key from her. We will trick her into coming here and bringing it with her.' He cackled with laughter at the sheer genius of his plan. He should have thought of it before.

'This is Mr Poley,' he said, phoning her at the hotel an hour later, 'from the warehouse . . .?'

'Oh aye. Hello, Mr Poley.'

'A terrible thing has happened to the Skimmer. Can you come along right away and bring the key for it?'

'What? What d'you mean?' Super Gran cried. 'What terrible thing's happened?'

'Oh . . . ah . . . um . . . you see . . .' Roly stammered, making it up as he went along, 'a man came to the warehouse and . . . ah . . . um . . . asked to see the Skimmer, and he . . .'

'A man . . .?' Super Gran cut in. 'A wee man? A worried-looking wee man, with two big bully-boys with him?' She still thought that Mr Fry was a baddie and that Roly was a goodie! How wrong could she be!

'Er . . . yes . . . that is the one,' Roly said.

Super Gran turned to the children beside her. 'It's that wee scunner — he's been after the Skimmer, so he has!'

This aside gave Roly time to think of some lies to tell her. And when she went back on to the phone again it gave Edison time to ask Willard: 'What *is* a scunner?'

'*I* dunno,' the boy shrugged. 'Somethin' Scottish, I suppose.'

Meanwhile, Roly was fibbing: 'He found a way of

by-passing your anti-theft device . . . and he took the Skimmer away . . .!'

'No!'

'Yes. And he . . . er . . . crashed it outside. But do not worry, dear lady, we managed to chase him off, and we are guarding it where it stands, out in the street.'

'Whew! That's a relief,' Super Gran breathed. 'But here, wait a minute! What d'you mean "we"? I thought your assistants were crooks?'

'Ah . . . yes . . . um . . . they are . . . that is, the two you saw are. But I've got other ones as well,' he lied. 'Anyway, could you come along, check the Skimmer for damage and bring the key to unlock the device. We cannot push the vehicle back into the warehouse otherwise.'

'Aye, of course,' Super Gran said, falling into the trap. 'I'll do that. Straight away.'

When she and the children arrived at the warehouse, they were surprised when they *didn't* see the Skimmer parked outside on the street.

'That's funny,' Edison said. 'I thought he said it had crashed out here somewhere?'

'Aye, lassie, he did.' Super Gran was puzzled, and suspicious.

They entered the warehouse through the small door at the side of the large double doors — and were amazed to see the Skimmer standing where they had left it, still covered by its white tarpaulin.

'What . . .? It's here! *And* there's nothing wrong with it, either!' Super Gran exclaimed, as she pulled a corner of the cover aside and saw that the vehicle was completely undamaged. 'What was that wee man blethering about, eh?'

'Dunno,' Willard muttered, scratching his head, as all three of them looked around the warehouse, which was full of boxes, crates and packing-cases, but empty of people.

'And where *is* everyone?' Edison asked, puzzled.

Super Gran looked suspicious. 'M'mm, I think there's something funny going on here. But I don't know what. Maybe I should try the Skimmer out, to make sure it's working, eh?' She took the key out of her handbag and walked towards the vehicle. 'Open up the big doors, Willie, so that we can get it out, will you?'

Suddenly, before Willard could open the doors, or before she could take another step nearer the Skimmer, the Pole and the Punk shot out of their hiding-place behind a stack of large crates of foodstuffs, where they had been lying in wait.

'Yah-ah-ah . . .!' yelled the Punk, thinking for the moment that he was a *Red* Indian – rather than a *Pink* Punk!

'Gimme that key!' the Pole demanded, as he tried to snatch it out of Super Gran's hand.

Roly, who still didn't want Super Gran to know that he was a crook and who was staying well out of sight of this key-grabbing session, had thought it would be easy for his men to take the key from Super Gran. But it wasn't as easy as all that! For what they didn't realize was that her Super-powers hadn't faded altogether, they just came and went a bit. They faded and returned. And, at the moment, they had returned!

'Gimme it!' the Punk yelled, as he and the Pole tried to wrench it out of her hand. But her other hand promptly biffed each of them in turn in the eye, with a rapid 'biff, biff'.

'Ouch! Ugh!' they cried, but hung on and continued to struggle with her.

'Run!' Super Gran shouted to the children. 'Get out of here. It was a trap!'

They scampered out through the door, but looked back to see if Super Gran was following. She was. At least, she was trying to! For the two baddies were hanging on to her, trying to prise the key from her fingers.

'Get off, you wee scunners! You're not getting it, so there!'

'Gimme it!' the Pole demanded again — and got her fist on his nose! Super Gran, they had found, wasn't as weak as she was supposed to be!

'You'd better watch out,' the Punk warned her, nodding towards the Pole, 'he's got a black belt. He's an expert in judo!'

'Humph!' she snorted. 'Judo? An expert in *ludo* is more like it!'

She thumped the Pole's stomach with her elbow, then followed up — with the piston-like forward movement of her arm — with a jab of her bony little fist into the Punk's stomach.

'Ouch! Ow!' they chorused.

With each of them doubled over, she got the chance

to escape through the door into the street outside. But not for long! For they shot out after her, carrying the fight out there.

'Come on!' Willard urged Edison, as he jumped on the Pole's back to help Super Gran fight him.

Edison did the same to the Punk, although she wasn't quite sure what good it would do, reckoning she'd be about as much of a nuisance to the man as an ant would be to an elephant! However, she held on grimly round his neck, hoping that she might be choking him a little bit!

Suddenly, in the midst of this struggle, it happened! The Punk managed to knock the key out of Super Gran's hand. There was a loud 'plop' – and all five of them stopped struggling and looked down at the drain grating into which the key had fallen!

So that was that. Now *none* of them had it . . .!

9 How (Not) to Drive a Skimmer!

After a moment's horrified silence, Super Gran's temper shot up to boiling-point – and she went berserk! 'You rotten wee bachles, you!' Her temper improved her Super-powers and she lashed out wildly at her enemies.

The men threw the children off their backs – which was just as well! – before Super Gran battered them like a tartan tornado, until the baddies decided that they'd had enough and ran off – or rather, limped hurriedly away! – to go and fetch some of their big, tough, crooked pals to give them a hand!

'Thought you said she'd lost her rotten powers?' the Pole protested as he hobbled away. 'You're jokin'!'

'Don't understand it,' the Punk moaned, limping along. 'She *had* lost 'em, honestly.'

Super Gran and the children, watching the men run off, didn't turn to look at the warehouse behind them. If they had done, they would have seen an extremely disappointed Roly, who had sneaked out of his hiding-place and was now peeking out at them round the edge of the warehouse door.

'Well, at least if *we* do not have the key to unlock the Skimmer,' he muttered to himself, 'then neither does she. And *I* can get the Pole's friend, "Keys" Stone, to *make* a key, before *she* can do anything about it.'

But Roly was wrong!

'Well, that's it!' Edison said. 'That's the key lost. So we won't be able to move the Skimmer now. Not until Dad can make another one.'

But Super Gran had an idea. 'Oh, I don't know about that, lassie,' she grinned, 'I think *I* know how we could move it.'

'What're you goin' to do, Gran?' Willard asked eagerly.

'Come on, I'll show you!' she replied, turning back towards the warehouse — just *after* Roly had ducked back inside, out of sight behind a packing-case, wondering what she was up to now.

They entered the warehouse and Super Gran climbed up into the Skimmer. 'Now that I've got my strength back, at least for the time being . . .'

'Yes,' Edison agreed, interrupting, 'it *does* rather seem to come and go, doesn't it?'

'I reckon,' Super Gran continued, 'that I might just be able to pull the steering wheel out from the dashboard, hold it there and steer the Skimmer. See . . .?' She pulled it and, as she said, she *did* have enough strength to hold it out and turn it to guide the vehicle.

But there was a problem! In order to do this, she had to press her feet against the dashboard and lean right back at full stretch, until she was lying flat on her back along the length of the driving-seat — which was in its 'reclined' position. And from there she couldn't see out of the windscreen!

'*And* I can't reach the gear-lever or the foot-pedals

either,' she complained. 'Och! It's no use! I couldn't drive like this. Forget it!'

'*I'll* work the gears and the pedals for you, Gran!' Willard volunteered eagerly. He had been dying to drive the Skimmer – and here was his big chance!

He clambered into the cabin beside his Gran, into a position where he could reach the controls. But to do this he had to crouch down on the Skimmer's floor to use all his strength on them, so that he too was unable to see out of the windscreen. So this meant that neither of them could see to steer the Skimmer. There was nothing else for it – Edison would have to help them!

So, after she had opened the warehouse's large doors to let the Skimmer out, Edison joined the others in the cabin to act as their 'eyes'. And to do this she had to perch, kneeling, on the front passenger seat.

Roly, from his hiding-place, saw the Skimmer start up and drive slowly out of the warehouse, across the main road and on to the common. Then he sneaked out to see what would happen – with three drivers aboard!

At first Super Gran and company managed not too badly. But then, once they reached the common and tried to manoeuvre it around on the wide open spaces, they discovered that there was more to driving a vehicle with three drivers than they imagined!

For a start, Edison didn't know her right from her left. And the first they knew of it was when they were heading towards a tree!

'Go right a bit, Super Gran,' she instructed. Adding,

when the instructions were carried out: 'Go right! Right, I said! Quickly – look out, the tree . . .!'

'But I *am* going right,' Super Gran insisted.

'I mean left,' Edison hurriedly corrected. 'Go left! Left . . .!'

Super Gran turned the wheel just in time, although the Skimmer grazed the tree, bumping them all about the cabin.

'Whew! That was a near thing,' Edison sighed. 'You went the wrong way there.'

'*I* went the wrong way?' Super Gran gasped. 'I just did what you told me! Humph! Cheek!'

And things didn't improve. They spent the next half-hour skimming over the common, dodging a pond, bushes, passers-by, a statue of a local mayor – and a little white poodle sniffing around the bushes.

'Typical! Trust her!' Willard muttered disgustedly from the Skimmer's depths after more of Edison's bad direction, such as:

'Turn left . . . no, I mean right . . . no, left . . .'
– causing the Skimmer almost to crash into a large clump of shrubbery.

In addition to this, Super Gran found that her Super-strength was running out on her again and she momentarily lost her grip on the steering wheel. She grasped it again almost instantly, but not before she had lost control for a few seconds – causing the vehicle to make an accidental U-turn.

Meanwhile, the Pole and the Punk were returning to the warehouse with six 'heavies' – large, burly, tough guys to help them put Super Gran to flight. At the

edge of the common they met Roly, who told them to get after the Skimmer, last seen skimming amongst the trees.

So the gang rushed on to the common to chase after the Skimmer — which then did its U-turn and came straight for them!

The gang — as one man! — ran in the opposite direction. And then, as the Skimmer reached them, skimming low over them, they threw themselves on the ground — to avoid being beheaded!

The vehicle, now out of control because of Super Gran's failing strength (and Edison's bad direction!), veered to the side and circled around, causing great confusion in the gang's ranks. They just didn't know what to do to dodge it!

'Hey! Give over!' the Pole yelled, scared, as the Skimmer, heading in the direction of the warehouse, swooped low over him.

Finally, Super Gran's Super-strength ran out altogether and the Skimmer crash-landed on the grass, skittering across it like a giant drunken frisbee!

She and the children climbed out.

'Look!' Willard pointed behind them to where, in the distance, the baddies were running towards them.

'Quick!' Super Gran urged the children. 'Run!'

'But what about the Skimmer?' Edison asked. 'Those crooks'll get it!'

'Don't worry, lassie,' Super Gran gasped as she ran, 'we'll tell the police about it.'

But she didn't have to. For just then they met Roly, waddling slowly after his men.

'Do not concern yourself, dear lady,' he had the presence of mind to say. 'I still have some influence over my assis – er . . . *former* assistants. Do not worry. They will listen to me.'

Super Gran felt ashamed about running away from a fight and leaving the Skimmer behind. But she consoled herself that on this occasion, outnumbered as they were, flight was the only thing for it. And, still thinking that Roly was a goodie, she believed that the Skimmer would be safe with him.

When the gang reached the vehicle, now dented and looking the worse for wear, Super Gran and company were far enough away to be safe.

'Never mind them,' the Pole said, 'what about this?' He pointed to the Skimmer. 'What do we do with it?'

He got his answer when Roly reached them, puffing and panting and wobbling like an overweight blancmange. He had seen how Super Gran had been able to drive it with a little help from her friends, and he reckoned whatever *they* could do, he and his gang could do too!

'You two . . . puff, pant,' he gasped, nodding towards the Pole and the Punk, 'should be able to drive it . . . puff, pant . . .' He explained how Super Gran and the children had driven it. 'It should be easy . . . puff, pant . . . If *she* can do it, now that she is weak, then you two can . . . puff, pant . . .!'

'Weak?' the Pole muttered, nursing his numerous bruises. 'You're jokin'!'

The two men climbed aboard the Skimmer, and

each of them in turn tried to pull the wheel out. But neither of them was strong enough.

'Huh!' snorted the Punk as he hauled unsuccessfully on the wheel. 'If she's supposed . . . to be weak . . . how can she . . . pull this . . . rotten wheel . . . out and . . . turn it . . . huh?'

So it was decided that *both* men were needed just to pull it out! Which meant that Roly had to be hoisted bodily up and inside the vehicle, to do what Willard and Edison had done — work the controls and give directions to the two drivers.

At least Roly, being taller than Willard, was able to see where they were going. The trouble was, with *two* drivers instead of one, each of them thought that Roly's directions concerned only *him*! So that when he said, 'Turn to the right, a little bit' — each of them turned the wheel to the right a little bit, which made *two* little bits that the Skimmer turned — which was too much! And so once again the vehicle zigzagged about wildly!

It was rather crowded in the cramped cabin with three full-grown men in it. (One of whom, Roly, was round and extremely fat!) Each of them wanted more room for himself! And they never did learn to coordinate their movements or to cooperate with each other, so you can imagine how the Skimmer ran amok again all over the common!

Not only did they keep bumping into trees, bushes and the mayor's statue, but they narrowly avoided a certain little white poodle, still sniffing around the bushes — making it run for its life!

Eventually, when they crash-landed, it was decided

that other arrangements would have to be made for using the Skimmer as a getaway car.

'We'll just have to capture that there Super Gran,' the Punk suggested, 'an' make *her* drive it for us.'

'Yeah,' the Pole added, 'or wait till "Keys" makes a key for it. He's working on it now.' 'Keys' Stone, a friend of the Pole, was an expert on keys, locks and lock-picking.

'Then while "Keys" is working on it, *I* shall be thinking of a way to capture her,' Roly decided, as his gang, plus their six 'heavy mob' friends, pushed the Skimmer back to the warehouse. 'But we shall have to hurry — for the "big job" is due in two days' time . . .!'

10   Posh Nosh

'The Skimmer's safe. Roly's just phoned me,' Super
Gran told the children as she joined them at their
dining-room table that evening for dinner. 'He managed somehow to get it back to the warehouse.'

'That's good news,' Edison replied as the waiter
served them and Willard grabbed his knife and fork
desperately.

'Oh,' Super Gran added, 'I forgot to ask him about
that mysterious phone call about the Skimmer being
damaged and left out in the street.'

'You can ask him next time he phones,' said Edison
as, disgusted, she watched Willard eating.

The boy was enjoying his hotel food; especially since
it was fancier than the food he got at home. 'Wow!
This is . . . scrumptious,' he spluttered, between
mouthfuls. 'Scrumpy!' He spurted bits of chicken,
mushroom, tomato, egg, cray-fish and parsley all over
the place as he ate – and spoke!

'Just *look* at him!' Edison said, trying *not* to look at
him! 'Stuffing himself as if the waiter was going to
whip it away again!'

'Well . . . you never . . . know!' Willard retorted.
'An' it's scrumpy! Scrumpy-ma-humpy!'

'Yes, so you said!' Edison remarked drily.

'M'mm,' Super Gran agreed, 'it certainly is lovely

food we're getting here. But I'm not used to the fancy food, and the sweets and trifles! I hope it doesn't upset my tummy.'

'It *is* rather rich, isn't it?' Edison said. 'I think it's what they call "posh nosh".'

'Aye lassie, it's certainly a big difference from *my* usual fare — porridge, fish and chips, mince and "tatties", custard and . . .'

'Porridge!' Edison practically threw her knife and fork on to the table in her excitement.

'Huh?' Super Gran was taken aback. But Willard, too busy eating, ignored the girl.

'Porridge!' Edison repeated. 'Maybe that's it!'

Super Gran looked down at her plate, then looked at the menu in front of her. 'Dinna be daft, lassie; it's not porridge — it's Chicken Marengo!'

'No, I don't mean *that*!' Edison explained. 'Tell me, Super Gran, are you still taking porridge for breakfast?'

'Well . . . no, I'm not. Not since we've been living it up in this posh hotel.'

'That's it, then!' Edison almost shouted in triumph.

'What's it then, hen?' Super Gran asked, puzzled.

'You haven't been eating porridge every morning, the way you always do at home. Right?' Super Gran nodded silently as she ate. 'And you normally have it *every* morning, don't you? You told me, *and* those reporters at the exhibition, that you couldn't do without it.'

Super Gran nodded again.

'You "*couldn't do without it*",' Edison emphasized. 'See? That's what's causing you to lose your Super-powers. You need porridge every day to make sure you keep them.'

'Och lassie, that's nonsense!' Super Gran smiled. 'Blethers! It was yon Super-ray that made me Super, not porridge!'

'Yes,' Edison agreed, 'but maybe it works *along with* the ray, to *keep* you Super. And when you stopped eating it, your Super-powers faded a bit? Couldn't that be it?'

'Aye . . . well . . . I don't know . . .'

'Or maybe it's that rich food you've been eating,' Edison went on, getting carried away now. 'Or maybe it's the two of them together? Eating rich food and *not eating* porridge?' Edison was convinced that she was right.

'Don't listen to her, Gran,' Willard cut in, spluttering food in all directions. 'She's talkin' a load of rubbish!'

'All right,' Edison challenged, 'why don't you try eating porridge again, and *not* eating this "posh nosh" — and see if it works? See if your Super-powers return? How about it?'

'Just ignore her, Gran,' Willard advised. 'She's potty!'

'I'm *not* potty, *you're* potty . . .'

'No I'm not . . .'

Super Gran, looking down at her half-finished meal, was wondering if Edison could possibly be right. *Should* she stop eating all this and start eating porridge again? Naturally, she was reluctant to do so. After all, this was the first time in her life that she'd had the chance to eat 'posh nosh' — and Mr Silver and the exhibition were paying for it. It wasn't as if *she* could afford it, or would ever be able to afford it.

Still, if it meant getting her Super-powers back again . . . What was more important, a few fancy meals — or her Super-powers? There was only one answer!

'Right then, lassie,' she agreed, as she took another forkful of food, 'I'll start first thing tomorrow, at breakfast, with my usual porridge . . .'

'Oh no you won't, Super Gran!' That wasn't what Edison had in mind! She whipped away the old lady's plate from right under her poised knife and fork, then she turned and shouted across the dining-room: 'Waiter! I say — waiter . . .!'

'Yes . . . er, madam . . .?' The waiter bowed, looking at Super Gran. But it was Edison who was giving the orders!

'Please take this away, will you . . .?'

The waiter, his hand out to take the plate, looked puzzled. What was the matter with it, he wondered? This was one of the best dishes that André, their master chef, made. He was proud of it. In fact, he would go bananas if anyone dared send it back with a complaint! And he was liable to blow his top at him, Jimmy the waiter, for being the unfortunate one chosen to convey the dish, and the bad news, to the kitchen.

'Och, don't worry, Jimmy,' Super Gran assured the astonished waiter, having read his mind. 'There's nothing wrong with it. I'm *sure* it's one of Andy's best dishes, he *should* be proud of it, he doesn't *have* to go bananas, we're *not* complaining — and if he blows his top at you, just tell him to see *me*, and I'll explain all about losing my Super-powers, and . . .'

The waiter stared. Baffled. How could this little old lady know all that? Or had he spoken aloud, he wondered?

'No, you didn't speak aloud, Jimmy,' she assured him again. 'I can read your mind, you see. That's one of the Super-powers I was telling you about, and . . .'

The man lifted her plate and reeled away towards the kitchen. Reading his mind? Super-powers . . .?

'Oh,' Edison called after him, 'and will you bring her a plate of porridge instead?'

'A p-p-plate of p-p-porridge?' The waiter looked back over his shoulder, unable to believe his ears. 'For dinner? In here?' It was unheard of!

Super Gran sighed. 'Aye, laddie. I've to start on porridge again — right away. For the sake of my Super-powers. Understand?'

The man understood nothing! Only that he was taking a sumptuous dish back to the kitchen, and he was to ask for porridge! At that time of night! It was unthinkable. André would kill him!

'Although I must say, lassie,' Super Gran said, rather peeved, 'you might at least have let me finish my Chicken Marengo, so you might! It wasn't much to ask.'

'But if it *is* the lack of porridge,' Edison explained, 'then the sooner you start the better.'

'Aye, but — porridge at dinner-time? At *this* time of night? My stomach'll never stand it. It's used to having its ration of porridge at eight o'clock in the morning

— not at eight o'clock in the evening! It won't know what's hit it, so it won't!'

Edison made a face, as if to say, 'I'm not going to argue with you, it's for your own good!' Then she calmly resumed her meal, eating the food that she was denying Super Gran!

But if Edison and Super Gran thought that the waiter would bring her porridge, just like that — they were wrong. For the only thing the waiter brought was — André, the master chef! And André was anything but pleased!

' 'Oo ees zis peoples 'oo make ze complaints about André? Huh? Ware are zey?' he demanded, as he stamped through the dining-room.

Jimmy the waiter pointed to Super Gran's table. Then he stood back and, being a waiter, he waited — to see what would happen!

'Och, don't get your sporran in a fankle!' Super Gran smiled. 'We're not complaining. Your food's great. Fabulous!'

'Scrumpy!' Willard, still eating messily, chipped in.

'Then wot is ze complaints, uh?' André demanded, his face flushed scarlet at the very idea of a diner actually criticizing his food. 'No one, *no* one effer complaints about ze food de André!' He broke into a torrent of French which sounded as if he were swearing at them, his tall white chef's hat wobbling with his anger.

'It's just that we . . . er . . . want . . . um . . . porridge,' she said.

'Porridge? You're flippin' well not on, mate!' the

chef yelled. His anger made him forget he was supposed to be French, and he suddenly changed from the French 'André' to his usual English 'Andy' — which Super Gran had known all about from reading the waiter's mind. 'Not at this ruddy time of night. No way. You're not on. Forget it!'

The man just wouldn't listen when Super Gran explained why she had to have porridge, and why *then*, instead of waiting until the next morning's breakfast. He merely threw a tantrum and, remembering that he was supposed to be French, he threw it in broken French!

'Non! Ze keetchen staff, zey vill not make ze porreedge at zis time of ze even-ing. Non, non, non!'

Super Gran sighed and put her hands up to her temples (which sometimes helped to get results, especially now when her powers were coming and going). She read a bit of André/Andy's mind — and decided to blackmail him! There was nothing else for it!

She beckoned him to bend down closer to her, so that no one else would hear, and whispered: 'I'm sorry about this, Andy, honestly, but if you don't bring me some porridge right away — I'll be forced to tell the manager about you . . .!'

'About *me*? About ze André?' he said snootily, looking down at her haughtily. 'Tell him wot about ze André, uh?' He put on a smug look. He was sure of himself. What could a little old lady tell the manager about *him*?

'I could tell him about you helping yourself . . .'

'Helping myself?' He still looked smug and confident.

'Aye, helping yourself to foodstuffs from the kitchen — every week. And selling them outside, to your friends, relations and . . .'

André/Andy went deadly white. His confidence vanished instantly — like Willard devouring a trifle! — and he turned and ran to the kitchen!

'Well, Super Gran, I don't know what you said to that chef,' Edison said later as the old lady tucked into a large plate of porridge, 'but whatever it was, it certainly did the trick!'

Super Gran, slurping up her porridge, smiled at the children in turn. 'Ah, that's between me and Andy . . . I mean, André! That's *our* little secret.'

But if Super Gran thought that that was all the porridge she was going to have to take that day, she was mistaken. For later, up in their suite, Edison insisted on phoning down to 'room service' — to have a plateful sent up for the old lady's supper!

Next morning, Super Gran had more porridge, for breakfast, which was only to be expected. But Edison then insisted on her having a huge helping — at lunchtime! (At the exhibition centre's canteen.) *And* for dinner that evening — for the second night running! So poor old Super Gran, who never thought that she would ever feel like that about it, was beginning to dislike the very thought of porridge!

But she consoled herself that Edison might be right. For she definitely felt herself getting stronger, with her Super-powers returning. And, when her strength was back, it was back for longer periods at a time.

That evening after dinner, however, Willard saw someone who brought their minds back from Super Gran's porridge problems to other problems.

While he was strolling through the hotel foyer, he caught sight of the Pole, lurking about behind a large potted palm — obviously up to something.

'I'm going along there,' Super Gran declared, when Willard reported this, 'to read that Pole's mind. That is, if he's got a mind! I'm going to find out what's going on!'

'Maybe we should come along and help you, in case you get into any trouble?' Edison offered, remembering that the old lady's Super-powers hadn't *quite* come back to full strength yet.

'Jings, lassie, who d'you think I am? I'm Super Gran, and I can do *any* . . .' She stopped before completing her usual boast, remembering that just then she wasn't *too* Super. 'Och, don't panic. I'll look after myself.'

But, as it turned out, she didn't *have* to look after herself. For there was no sign of the Pole in the foyer. By the time she got there, he was gone.

However, that didn't stop Edison worrying. For she reckoned that sooner or later both groups might make another attack on Super Gran — who was *still* nothing like her usual Super self.

'Super! That's it!' she cried. 'Tub! Super Tub! We could get Tub to come up to London and give you a hand, Super Gran!'

'What? Get Tub to help *me*?' She was indignant. 'Havers!'

This time, Edison could not persuade Super Gran to listen to her. So the girl took things into her own hands. Taking her purse downstairs to the public phone booth in the foyer so that the other two wouldn't know what she was up to, she phoned Tub. She told him all about Super Gran's fading Super-powers, and the troubles they were having with the Skimmer and the various lots of baddies, and she asked him if he could come up and help them.

'Yeah, sure,' Tub said. 'I'll ask the boss for time off me work.'

Edison gave him the address of the hotel, rang off and left the phone booth, wondering if Super Gran would be annoyed at her. She was so busy with her thoughts that she didn't notice the two figures who crept up behind her until it was too late!

While one of them threw a sack over her head and hustled her out of a fire exit into a waiting car, the other one lingered momentarily in front of a hotel mirror, to comb his greasy hair and admire the pink reflection which smiled back at him. Then he hurried out into the night to catch up with his mate, the Pole, and Edison — their captive!

11 Captured!

'Whatever's happened to that lassie?' asked Super Gran. 'She's been gone for ages. And where was she going, anyway?'

'Dunno,' replied Willard, too busy watching television.

In answer to her, the phone rang. It was Roly — to tell her that the girl had been kidnapped and was being held at the warehouse.

'So, if you know what is good for you, you will come along here with the boy. And you will not contact the police — or else . . .' He slammed the phone down.

'So! That wee fat podge *is* a baddie!' she cried. 'I wondered about him. And now he's kidnapped Edison!'

'Huh! Trust her to go and get herself kidnapped!' Willard muttered. 'What are you goin' to do?'

'We've no choice. We'll have to do as he says, the bachle!'

At the hotel reception desk they left the address of the warehouse, so that they could be contacted.

When they arrived there and joined Edison, Roly fastened a pair of police handcuffs on Super Gran's wrists to make sure that she couldn't use her Superstrength on him or his men.

'Now,' he addressed her, feeling safer, 'are you going to help us?'

'What with?'

'The Skimmer?'

'In what way?'

'To drive it. Or fly it. Or whatever it is you do with it!'

'Away, you wee baldy scunner! Drive it yourself! Or get your gang of thugs there to drive it!' She knew that they'd probably never manage to drive it the way she and the children had done.

'*We* cannot hold the wheel out,' Roly admitted, 'but *you* can. So are you going to help us or not?'

'That's right!'

'You are?' he beamed.

'I'm *not*!'

He scowled. 'Right, you can stay here until I get a key made to unlock that confounded device.'

'Stay here?' Edison cried. 'For how long?'

'Until it is safe for me to let you go,' Roly smiled.

The Pole led him aside and whispered: 'The "big job", boss . . .?'

'Ah! Yes . . .' Roly looked at his watch for the date. 'Yes, you are right, Beanpole. The "big job" is the day after tomorrow. So "Keys" will have to get a move on, or else we shall have to make other arrangements.'

He went over to his office, yanked the telephone wires out of the wall and carried the instrument away. 'Just in case you were thinking of telephoning the police!' He smirked as he proceeded with his gang towards the warehouse door. 'We shall see you in a day or two. We have things to arrange.'

'You're not leaving us here *that* long?' Edison said, aghast.

'Without food?' Willard said, even more aghast!

'Oh, do not worry.' Roly gestured all around the packed warehouse. 'There is probably some food about somewhere,' he laughed. 'If you can find any, you are welcome to it! And there is even a cooker, over there!' He pointed to two small rooms next to the office, against the side wall of the warehouse.

'Don't worry, Gran,' Willard blurted out defiantly, 'Mr Silver'll soon miss you and he'll check at the hotel, and we told *them* we were comin' here . . .' Too late he realized that he had given the show away!

Roly swung round from the door, gloating. 'Well *that* will not do you much good! For *I* phoned Mr Silver before you got here and told him that you had to leave for home in a hurry. *And* I contacted the hotel, too. And told them that you were checking out and that I would be along right now to collect your luggage!'

Highly pleased with himself, he sniggered nastily, stepped out through the door – and locked it behind him.

They were trapped!

But there was always Tub, thought Edison. Could *he* rescue them?

Then she remembered that she hadn't given him the address of the warehouse. So they *were* trapped!

'At least we can get some *food*,' said Willard, getting his priorities right!

But when they looked round at the hundreds of

crates, packing-cases, boxes and cartons which were stacked round the walls from floor to ceiling, they realized that there wasn't much indication on most of them to say what food they contained; if, indeed, they contained food at all.

Willard searched for something like a crowbar to open the crates. But all he could find was a pen-knife, which was only good for opening a carton of chocolate – which suited Willard!

'Huh! You'll soon get tired of eating chocolate!' Edison said.

'Who will! Just watch me!' grinned Willard, munching happily.

'Aye, there must be something more substantial somewhere,' Super Gran said, as she struggled unsuccessfully to free herself from the handcuffs. 'Tch! If only I could get these off . . .'

Edison too began snooping around, reporting back that she had inspected the two little rooms beside the office. One was a toilet and the other was a small kitchen with a sink and a cooker, so they'd be able to cook some food – if only they could get into the crates to find it!

'I haven't enough strength just now to break these handcuffs,' Super Gran said, 'but I might just have enough strength in my legs.'

'What for?' Edison asked her.

'Come over here and I'll show you.' Super Gran walked to a nearby crate. She lifted her right foot and swung her leg back as far as she could.

'What are you doing?' Edison asked.

Super Gran swung her leg forward, hard, at the crate.

'Oh!' Edison cried out. 'Careful, Super Gran! You'll hurt yourself!'

'Blethers, lassie!' she said, as her foot made contact with the front of the crate — and smashed it open. 'I just *knew* I had a bit of strength in my legs, see?'

Willard rushed forward, pulled away the broken spars and fought his way into the crate. Then, 'Ugh!' he muttered, bringing out — one in each hand — two packets of porridge oats. 'Yeugh! That's all we need!'

'Yes!' Edison yelled excitedly. 'That *is* all we need. Porridge! Don't you see? Porridge — for Super Gran. To help her build up her strength . . .!'

'Oh no!' Super Gran groaned. 'In here? Porridge? That's the only reason I was happy to be imprisoned here — to get *away* from porridge!'

'But Super Gran,' Edison said, 'I thought you *liked* porridge.'

'Aye lassie, I *did*! But I've had so much of it in the last few days — and for every meal too! — that I'm just about sick of the stuff!'

'But you'll need to keep taking it, to get your Super-powers fully back to normal,' Edison pointed out.

'Oh, I suppose so.' Super Gran moped, then brightened. 'But I couldn't eat *raw* porridge! Even *you*, lassie, wouldn't make me eat raw porridge oats, would you?'

Edison grinned. 'That's no problem. The little kitchen, remember? We'll be able to cook it for you!'

Super Gran groaned again. More porridge! There

was no way out for her. If she wanted her Super-powers back permanently, she knew that she'd have to persevere with it. So she gritted her teeth and watched Edison taking a large packet of the oats to the kitchen to prepare it.

Willard, for his part, utterly refused to have anything to do with porridge and insisted, after he and Edison had fed some of it to Super Gran, that the old lady went along a line of crates and kicked her way into more of them to see what they contained. Surely, he reckoned, there *must* be something better than porridge in *some* of them. They couldn't *all* be full of porridge? But what if they were? Horrors!

However, his luck was in. The crates which she kicked open contained such goodies as crisps, cakes, chocolate biscuits and sweets, as well as tins of cooked meats, potatoes and fruit.

So they settled down to enjoy themselves. Or at least, the children did. Poor old Super Gran — for her own good! — was forced to eat nothing but porridge!

Next day they went on helping themselves to the food from the crates (with Super Gran still on porridge, of course) for their breakfast, lunch, tea and supper — the whole day. With no sign of Roly and his gang returning.

On the second day Super Gran, by now heartily sick of the sight of porridge, found that she had enough strength in her wrists to be able to break out of the handcuffs.

'Look!' she exclaimed as she snapped them. 'I'm free!'

But she wasn't free for long!

For minutes later Roly and company returned, along with the six 'heavies', who were again needed to help move the Skimmer; this time *out* of the warehouse, into the street.

'Oh no!' Roly gasped, seeing Super Gran's broken handcuffs. 'They're ruined! A good pair of police handcuffs ruined!'

Then, while the Pole fetched a new pair from the office and the Punk and the 'heavies' guarded Super Gran until they were fastened on, Roly looked around at all the crates which had been smashed.

'And just look at the mess you have made of those! Tch!' He scowled, thinking of all the money he was losing through the food being eaten instead of being sold. This seemed to be all that was bothering him! He was going to make millions of pounds from today's 'big job', but that didn't stop him niggling over a few lost profits — from goods which they had hi-jacked in the first place! Not to mention a pair of handcuffs — which they'd nicked from a police 'nick'!

Then he remembered that he wouldn't have to sell anything ever again. Once they'd done the 'big job', he would be able to retire from business altogether and turn to full-time crime. Or, better still, he might be able to retire to South America and live on the proceeds.

But first things first. And the first thing was the Skimmer. 'Tell me, Super Gran,' he said, 'have you changed your mind?'

'What about?' She had read his mind as he had been thinking all this, and had got some idea of his plans.

'About driving the Skimmer for us.'

'What for? As a getaway car for your "big job"?'

He laughed. 'You must have been reading my mind . . .' He stopped. She *had* been reading his mind! He frowned and walked away to go into conference with his gang — *out* of range of her mind-reading powers!

But he forgot about her Super-hearing and Super-eyesight. For, although he was a good distance away from her, Super Gran was able to 'tune in' her hearing and 'zoom in' her Super-eyesight to where he stood at the other end of the warehouse. And she was able to hear and lip-read part of what he said, which was:

'. . . "big job" . . . taking place . . . two hours . . . at tower . . . Where is . . . "Keys" with key? . . . if not here soon . . . shall have to . . . do job . . . without Skimmer . . .'

Super Gran, knowing that her Super hearing and seeing powers had improved and that she was capable of breaking her handcuffs, wondered if her Super-strength had sufficiently improved to let her tackle the whole gang alone. Or wasn't she *that* strong yet? After all, she would be up against nine men!

However, before she could do anything about it, two things happened which put it out of her mind.

Firstly, 'Keys' arrived — at last — with the key he'd made for the Skimmer. So Roly brightened, his face beaming. This was more like it. His troubles were over! On with the 'big job'! (And this gave Super Gran *ten* men to tackle now!)

Secondly, the door burst open dramatically.

'Look!' Super Gran pointed with her handcuffed hands. 'It's that worried-looking wee man again.'

'Stop! Stand still, everyone! I'm Mr Fry — from Department Y,' he called out timidly, but trying to do it the way he'd seen it done on the telly! 'I'm here to take charge . . .'

The dramatic effect was spoiled by his large, burly henchmen (he had four with him this time), who, having a tendency to rush about a lot, did the same again! Hearing him say 'charge' — they charged!

They rushed forward into the warehouse, knocked him over, sent him sprawling on to the floor and trampled him underfoot — all four of them!

'Department Y?' said Super Gran, the light beginning to dawn.

'Just because that's what it's called, that's why!' replied Mr Fry in a mumble, from under his heap of men on the floor.

The little government man, having got nowhere with his phone calls to Super Gran and suspecting that Roly was deliberately being evasive about the Skimmer, had returned to the warehouse with four men and a lorry, determined, once and for all, to take charge of the vehicle for government and army tests. But he found that he and his men could not easily do this — from a lying position, in a heap on the floor!

Meanwhile, Roly was giving *his* men their instructions. 'Get them, men! Tie them up!' he commanded.

Within minutes there were eight people all sitting on the floor: Mr Fry and his four henchmen, Super Gran and the children — all tied up (or handcuffed) — and helpless . . .!

12   Warehouse Wars

Mr Fry, more nervous and worried-looking than ever, turned to Super Gran, sitting beside him. 'What's going on here? I came for the Skimmer. I'm from a government department, Department Y.'

'Ah!' she replied, 'I understand now. Y!'

'Well *I* don't understand Y, I mean why,' he said. 'And Y, I mean *why*, did you attack me and my men that time at the hotel?' He looked ready to burst into tears!

'We thought you were baddies,' she explained.

'We're most certainly not,' he complained.

While Super Gran was explaining that *his* men had started it, after all, by attacking *her*, Mr Fry interrupted:

'Look, they're opening the large doors. They're going to take the Skimmer away. And we're here to impound it . . .'

'Impound it?'

'I couldn't get hold of you, I kept phoning. And Poley kept lying to me about it; I knew he was up to no good. So we decided to impound it.'

'Impound it?' Super Gran repeated, horrified.

'Confiscate it – for army tests. The government want to take it over.'

Humph! That's what *you* think, thought Super Gran.

The large, high warehouse doors were now open. 'Keys' had placed the new key in the Skimmer's lock and Roly was trying to climb up into the cabin — with help from the Pole and the Punk, who were pushing and shoving him from below.

The gang was about to escape, to do their 'big job' — with the Skimmer.

Suddenly, a figure appeared at the open doors. A rather large, chubby figure, eating a sausage-roll; a somewhat weedy, spotty, harmless-looking teenager who said: 'Hi! I'm looking for Super Gran! The hotel people told me she was here. And *I'm* here to give her a helping hand with some baddies! I would've been sooner, but I couldn't get time off me work!' It was Tub. He added, as an afterthought: 'Is there a cafe hereabouts? I'm starving!'

At first there was utter silence, both from Roly's mob and from Mr Fry's men. And then, as one man, they burst out laughing. He was going to give Super Gran a helping hand with baddies, was he? The very idea! Tub didn't look as if he could give a helping hand to a kitten stepping up a kerb, never mind Super Gran in her present predicament — they thought!

But they didn't know that this wasn't just Tub. It was *Super* Tub!

'Give her a helping hand?' Roly sniggered. 'Fat chance! Fat? Ha ha! That is good — look at all *his* fat!' (Listen to who was talking about fat! Roly!)

'Fat?' Tub exploded, spluttering sausage-roll in all directions (reminding Edison of Willard's eating habits in their hotel dining-room!). '*I'm* not fat — it's muscles!'

'Muscles?' guffawed the Pole. 'My skinny, titchy two-year-old kid's got bigger muscles than that!'

Super Gran's voice suddenly rang out with the rallying cry: 'Get those rotten wee scunners, Tub laddie!'

And Tub, after gulping down the last bit of his sausage-roll (there was no point in wasting it, was there?), went into Super Tub action. 'Aieeeee . . .!' It was Tub's battle-cry!

Both Roly's baddies and Mr Fry's goodies thought they were imagining things. For the weedy-looking, spotty, chubby teenager had suddenly turned into a berserk, whirling dervish as he smashed his way in amongst the ten baddies, clobbering them right, left and centre, 'handing' out karate chops with his hands and 'footing' out kung fu kicks with his feet!

'Huh! Fat? *I'll* show you!' Tub muttered, tearing in at them.

'Ouch! Ow! Ooyah!' they yelled, as they got in the way of Tub's flying fists and feet.

'Ooooh-owww!' yelled Roly, as he got hit by a stray punch, fell over — and rolled away, on his ample fat, across the warehouse floor!

Super Gran, meantime, had snapped her way out of her latest pair of police handcuffs, causing Roly, when he stopped rolling, to murmur:

'Oh no! Not *another* pair of handcuffs gone!'

She jumped to her feet, dashed to Willard, unfastened his bonds and gave him hurried instructions: 'Untie Mr Fry's men, laddie. Then Mr Fry, then

Edison — in that order. And tell the men to join Tub and me!'

'Okay, Gran,' the boy said, eager to join the fray himself.

And so the sides in the battle gradually evened up. Or *more* than evened up, really, as first of all Super Gran joined Tub against the baddies, followed by Mr Fry's men, followed by Willard.

But *not* followed by Edison, who was not a fighter. And *not* followed by little Mr Fry — who was a fully paid-up member of the cowards' union!

However, the others were more than a match for Roly's gang and their friends, who were now wishing they hadn't come along in the first place!

Under cover of the fighting, Super Gran sneaked over to the Skimmer, forgotten for the moment in its corner. She climbed up to the cab, grabbed something from inside, jumped down again, dashed over to Edison — and stealthily handed the object to the girl. 'Here lassie, take this. Quick! Keep it safe!'

'What . . .?' Edison looked down at the thing in her hand, puzzled. Then she smiled and closed her fist over it.

'And get over there, out of the way,' Super Gran advised her, as she rejoined the battle, 'in case you get hurt.'

But as it turned out the fight was almost over. There was no one left to fight! The baddies were lying about all over the warehouse floor, nursing their injuries and counting their bruises.

'Okay, okay, we give up! Stop! Don't keep hitting

us!' one of the bigger toughies pleaded, as he lay there scowling up at Tub, who was towering over him. 'We give in. Honest!'

But while Super Gran and the others were 'dusting off their hands' and counting the 'bodies', Edison noticed that there were three missing! 'Roly, the Pole and the Punk are gone!' she exclaimed, realizing that they must have sneaked off during the battle.

'So!' Mr Fry said officiously, emerging from his cowering corner, his courage returned now that Super Gran and company had mopped up the baddies for him. 'So you've let those three escape, have you? They're wanted for obstructing a government department and it'll take us days to track them down again.'

'*I* let them escape? Well . . .!' Super Gran, for once, was speechless. The cheek of that wee scunnery man, she thought. After all we did for him, after saving him from the baddies. The cheek of him! Isn't that just like those wee government upstarts! Typical!

But then she realized something which put Mr Fry's cheek out of her mind. She realized that Roly and his 'gang of two' were probably away to carry out their 'big job' somewhere. Now, what was it they had said — something about a tower? But *which* tower? It could be anywhere. *And* the job was due to take place in under two hours' time!

Mr Fry cut in on Super Gran's thoughts by announcing that he was going to take charge of the Skimmer. 'You two' — he pointed to the biggest and broadest of his men — 'stand guard over it. You other two can take these hoodlums to the nearest police station, on the lorry. Meanwhile *I* shall take possession of the Skimmer's key.'

Roly's 'heavy mob' were herded on to the lorry which Mr Fry and company had brought for transporting the Skimmer, and were driven off.

Then one of the guards, who had climbed up to fetch the key out of the Skimmer's cab, announced: 'Hey Mr Fry, it's not here! Someone's nicked it!'

'Not there? It must be,' his boss argued. 'It was there a few minutes ago.'

'Poley must have taken it,' Mr Fry decided, after his guard had jumped down, repeated what he'd said and shrugged his shoulders. 'I'll have to phone the Department for further orders.' He walked purposefully towards the office.

'It's not working,' Edison pointed out. 'Roly disconnected it.'

But Mr Fry, being an officious government official, refused to listen to a mere child and ignored her. He soon found out she was right! 'Tch! I shall have to use a public phone box again.'

He turned to his men. 'While I'm gone, guard that vehicle with your lives. Understand?' He didn't trust Super Gran and company!

'Wait!' Super Gran said, as he marched towards the open doors. 'I overheard Roly talking about a "big job" somewhere, today — in two hours' time.' Mr Fry looked at her blankly. 'You know, a big robbery or something,' she explained.

'Or *some*thing?' he asked snootily. 'Don't you know?'

'No, laddie,' she snapped, 'he didn't exactly confide in *me*! But he did mention a tower . . .'

'Tower? What tower?' the man demanded irritably.

'As I said, laddie, he didn't actually confi — Wait a minute! A tower . . . *The* Tower! The Tower of London! The Crown Jewels! Maybe *that's* what he's after? He hopes to make millions of pounds out of the "big job", I know that!'

'Don't be ridiculous,' Mr Fry snapped, turning away. 'He couldn't possibly steal the Crown Jewels. Impossible. And besides, it's got nothing to do with *me*. It's not *my* department!'

'Maybe not,' Super Gran called after him, 'but surely you could do *something* about it? Tell the police or something? It's not *my* department either, if it comes to that!'

But Mr Fry, out in the street now, merely shrugged, unconcerned. '*You* tell the police. It's not my . . .'

'Department!' Super Gran added. 'No, so you said!'

She took Tub and the children into the office, away from the guards. 'We'll have to do something about Roly and his "big job",' she told them. 'Obviously that worried-looking wee man's not going to do anything about it.'

'Why don't you go to the police, Gran?' Willard asked.

'They wouldn't believe me,' she told him. 'Mr Fry didn't. We haven't any proof, you see. We don't know *where* it's taking place. It *might* be the Tower of London and the Crown Jewels — or it might be somewhere else altogether. We don't know. That was only a hunch on my part.'

'What'll we do then?' Tub asked, munching away on a bar of chocolate which Willard had given him — out of one of Roly's broken crates!

'There's only one thing we *can* do,' she replied, glancing out of the office door at the guards. 'We'll have to shoot across London to the Tower as quickly as possible and stop Roly's gang. *If* that's where they've gone.'

'And if it's *not* the Tower of London . . .?' Edison asked.

Super Gran shrugged. 'We'll just have to chance it, that's all.'

'But how are we goin' to shoot across London, Gran?' Willard asked, hoping that what *he* had in mind was what *she* had in mind. It was! The Skimmer!

'Aye, you're right, laddie,' she smiled, reading his mind. 'What else? That's the only thing that can get us there in time.'

'But will it get through the London traffic?' Edison asked doubtfully. 'And besides, you haven't got permission to use it on the public highway.'

'Humph! That's no problem, with what *I've* got in mind!' Super Gran told her.

'Does that mean we're goin' to fight the guards?' Willard asked, gesturing towards them.

'Yeah!' Tub boasted. 'Me and Super Gran can easily take on them two . . .'

'You mean,' Edison corrected Tub's grammar, ' "Super Gran and I" — and "those two"!'

126

'Eh?' the youth exclaimed, 'Super Gran and *you*?' He looked up and down Edison's slight figure. 'You're joking! And those two what?'

'No, I meant . . .' she began. 'Oh, never mind!'

'No, we're not going to attack the guards. Well, not *too* much, anyway! They're goodies, after all.'

'What then, Gran?' Willard asked.

'Tub'll distract them, while the rest of us sneak aboard with the key,' she explained.

'Hey! The key!' Willard remembered. 'It's missin'! Does that mean the *three* of us'll have to drive it again?' He glowered at Edison as he spoke. He didn't want to experience her attempts at helping to drive the Skimmer again. Not ever! If *she* was going to help to drive it then he, Willard, would rather walk to the Tower!

But Edison, as if *she* for once had done some mind-reading, opened her clenched fist to reveal, nestling in her now sweaty palm, the key which Super Gran had handed to her during the fight.

'The key!' Willard shouted. 'How did *you* get it?'

'Shhhhhh!' Edison shushed him, gesturing towards the guards. 'We don't want *them* to know about it!'

'I knew we'd need that key,' Super Gran explained, 'when yon wee Mr Fry told me he was going to impound the Skimmer. So I sneaked it out while everyone was busy fighting.'

'Yeah, but the guards?' Tub reminded them, pointing.

Not only was he desperate to tackle the guards, but he had also finished his chocolate bar! So he wanted either something else to eat — or some action to keep him busy!

'Right,' Super Gran said, drawing her fellow conspirators closer to her, 'here's what we'll do. You, Tub, will . . .'

13 Tub Puts His Foot Down!

Super Gran and the children left the office and headed straight for the open doors of the warehouse. 'We're off then,' the old lady called innocently to the guards as they passed.

'All right,' one of them called back. 'Cheerio!'

Just then Tub, who had been hanging about the office as if he wasn't with the others, suddenly let out a yell – his battle-cry again: 'Aieeeee . . .!'

Then he rushed at full speed towards the men – who were taken aback, to say the least! They remembered seeing him in action and what he had done to the baddies; they remembered how he had gone berserk. So what was he up to this time? How would they deal with him? *Could* they – only *two* of them – deal with him, when ten baddies hadn't been able to do too much about him earlier?

Then, as suddenly as the battle-cry had started, so it stopped – when Tub reached them and screeched to a halt right in front of them. They were even more puzzled. What was he up to *now*?

They soon found out!

Tub jumped – with his Super-strength – on the foot of each man: on the right foot of one, on the left foot of the other.

'Ow! Ouch! Ow-ow-ow!' the guards cried out in pain

as they hopped around — one hopping on his left foot, while the other hopped on his right! And each man clutched his numb, injured foot in his hand, nursing it, comforting it, coaxing it back to life again!

Meantime, instead of leaving the warehouse, Super Gran and the children had sneaked round the back of the Skimmer while Tub was distracting the guards' attention, and had climbed silently aboard.

Then, while the men hopped about in agony, Tub joined the others in the vehicle. Super Gran unlocked the steering wheel, started the engine and drove it out through the open warehouse doors.

'Hey!' one of the guards yelled as they ran after the Skimmer. 'Stop! Come back here!'

Or at least the guards *tried* to run after it. But, since each of them had a foot that was extremely tender, they could only limp painfully after the escaping vehicle! And with one man limping to his right side and the other limping to his left, they kept bashing into each other!

'Ouch! Watch it!'

'Ouch! *You* watch it!' they yelled at each other as they hobbled along.

As Super Gran steered the Skimmer to the left, Edison, looking to the right, saw Mr Fry coming back from phoning his boss.

He was astonished — and furious — to see the Skimmer escaping, and to see, limping along behind it, banging their shoulders together as they ran, his 'foot-sore' guards!

'Cheerio!' Edison waved to him cheerfully. But the man merely scowled and shook his little fist at them.

He was more worried-looking than ever, and his nervous moustache drooped dismally. What would his Department Y chiefs say when they heard that he had lost the Skimmer? 'Why?' they'd say. Not 'Y', but 'why'! And how? How had Super Gran managed to drive it away without the key? He'd never know!

Super Gran had decided, back in the warehouse office, that the best way through London for them — was along the River Thames! Not only would it be the quickest and safest way (being less congested than the roads), but it would also keep her from disobeying instructions, for they wouldn't be using the Skimmer on a public highway!

'The river?' Edison exclaimed, when Super Gran revealed her plans. 'But where *is* the river from here? Have you any idea?'

'Och, don't panic,' Super Gran laughed. 'We'll soon find it. It's a big river! And it's round about here somewhere!'

'D-d-do you think it'll float all right, Super Gran?' Edison asked timidly when they reached it and plunged down into the water.

'Of course it will, lassie,' she assured her. 'Didn't it float all right on yon boating-loch, back home?'

The safety of a shallow boating-lake was one thing, thought Edison, but the width — and depth! — of the murky River Thames was quite another! However, the Skimmer floated properly.

It responded to Super Gran's manoeuvres as they

weaved their way in and out of the other vessels on the river — vessels whose occupants could only stare in amazement at the Skimmer as it passed them on its way to the Tower.

But after a while Super Gran glanced at her watch. 'Oh-oh!' she murmured. 'We'll never get there in time at *this* rate.'

'Why don't we fly, Gran?' Willard suggested.

'That's what *I* was thinking,' she replied, as she applied the controls which made the Skimmer's wings extend, lifting the craft out of the water and into the air. 'Hold on! I'm going to give her all she's got!'

Needless to say, the sight of a *flying* Skimmer caused even more amazement amongst the other river-users than the sight of a mere floating Skimmer had done!

The familiar sight of London's Tower Bridge, now coming into view, gradually increased in size as the Skimmer approached it at its full air-speed.

'What do we do now, Super Gran?' Edison asked when they reached the bridge. 'Where do we go?'

The old lady replied by lifting the Skimmer a little bit higher into the air until it was at street-level beside the Tower of London and Tower Bridge. Then she turned it away from the river and landed it on the pavement outside the Tower, on the road which leads to Tower Bridge and runs between the Tower on one side and the World Trade Centre and St Katherine's Yacht Marina on the other.

Ignoring the astonished stares of passers-by and motorists who were witnessing what they thought was a UFO landing, they climbed out.

'Look, Gran!' Willard pointed excitedly to a car parked on the other side of the road a few hundred metres away, facing towards them and Tower Bridge.

It didn't require Super Gran's Super-eyesight to see that the splodge of pink sitting behind the steering-wheel was the Pink Punk!

'I was right!' Super Gran grinned. 'It *was* the Tower of London they were robbing. But surely not the Crown Jewels? Surely yon wee, fat, baldy man couldn't possibly hope to steal the Crown Jewels?'

'Let's get 'im!' urged Tub, thumping one fist into his other palm, spoiling for another fight.

'Look!' Edison pointed to a notice pasted on a hoarding near them. 'It says that the Crown Jewels of Swybia are on display at the Tower for a week, starting today.'

'Where's Swybia?' Willard asked.

'It's one of those new Arab states, isn't it, Super Gran?' Edison said.

'And it's *their* Crown Jewels that Roly's after!' the old lady cried. 'So that's it! While they're here on display!'

'But what about the Pink Punk?' Willard asked, pointing at the getaway car and the Punk — who was just at that moment getting away from it!

'Yes, come on,' Super Gran yelled. 'Let's get 'im!'

Roly and his gang, forced to do the famous 'big job' without the Skimmer, had had to steal a car for their getaway. While Roly and the Pole had entered the Tower to steal the Swybian Crown Jewels they had left the Punk in the car with the engine running.

But the Punk had spotted Super Gran and company before *they* had spotted him. After all, he had seen the Skimmer come up from the river, hover over the roadway and land across the street from him. He could hardly miss it! At first he had merely frozen with fright. But now that he'd had time to thaw out a bit — he was panicking! He saw them look in his direction, and point, and run towards him. So: the Punk — did a bunk!

Leaving the engine running in his blind panic, the man in pink opened the door, scrambled out and made a dash for freedom, heading in the general direction of St Katherine's Yacht Marina.

He didn't know where he was running to, but he fingered his bruises as he ran, the promise of others spurring him on! He didn't stop to think about who would drive the car for the getaway — he was only concerned now with his *own* getaway!

Super Gran, seeing the Punk escaping, went after the man, followed by Tub and Willard. But Edison, having tripped and fallen, was content to lag behind at her own pace.

With Super Gran and company in hot pursuit, the Punk ran along a road, inside the marina area and over a little road bridge, just as a yacht was approaching it, coming out of the haven to sail along the channel which leads to the Thames.

As Super Gran, behind him, reached the bridge, it started to open, lifting upwards into the air. The Punk, realizing that this would hinder the old lady, stopped running to turn and watch. Seeing the ever-increasing gap of the rising bridge, and the approaching yacht, and thinking that these were obstacles to the Super-running oldie, he grinned.

She would have to make a detour over a pedestrian bridge downstream to catch up with him. Or she would have to stop and wait for the bridge to be lowered again. Or, best of all, she wouldn't be able to stop and would plunge right into the channel! And serve her right!

He pulled his steel comb from his pocket to tidy up his greasy pink locks as he stood there, legs apart, grinning.

But there was no sign of Super Gran stopping. She came sprinting on, straight towards the rising bridge, the ever-widening gap, and the approaching yacht . . .!

14   Super Gran's for the High Jump!

The Pink Punk, of all people, should have known
better! After all, hadn't he witnessed Super Gran's
feats, not only at the exhibition but also at that wide
canal basin at Little Venice? So what was a little
obstacle like a yacht-channel and a rising bridge?

The Punk may have thought that Super Gran was
still powerless or that her jumping wasn't up to its old
standard. But of course he was wrong. For the little old
lady had eaten enough porridge in the last few days to
give her back her Super-powers fully and permanently.

So she merely sailed up into the air, and over the
gap and the approaching yacht — as if she had been
stepping over a puddle!

The Punk, aghast at this sight, forgot to turn and
run; once again he found himself rooted to the spot —
hypnotized!

On landing, Super Gran launched herself at him,
and in felling him she knocked the comb from his
hand into the water of the marina.

'Aw! Me comb!' he complained bitterly.

'Here, Tub,' Super Gran said, when he and Willard
had caught up with her, 'take this punky-monkey
along to the nearest policeman. And tell him he's one
of a gang stealing Swybia's Crown Jewels from that
display at the Tower. Oh, and tell him,' she added, as

Tub hurried the Punk away, with a wrestling arm-lock twisting the man's arm up his back, 'that Willard and I are off to pick up the others. Okay?'

While she and Willard hurried back towards the Tower to catch the others, Willard kept thinking about his gran's leap over the bridge-gap. Then he glanced up at Tower Bridge in the background, and sighed.

'I was just thinkin', Gran — that was some jump you did then!'

'Och! *That* was nothing.' She dismissed it modestly.

'I was just thinkin',' he repeated, glancing again at Tower Bridge, 'it would be even better if you could jump over *that* one, when it's openin'! Like that car did on the telly the other night. Remember?'

'Aye, but . . .' Super Gran began, when Edison interrupted her.

The girl came running towards them from the road where the getaway car was parked. She was waving her arms to attract their attention, and shouting.

'What is it, lassie?'

'I've just seen . . . puff, pant . . . Roly and . . . puff, pant . . . the Pole. Running out of the Tower . . . puff, pant . . . with a large sack each . . . the jewels! The car . . . puff, pant . . .!'

'Don't worry! I'll get the wee scunners!' Super Gran yelled, as she zoomed away along the road to catch the crooks, leaving the children to follow her.

Roly and the Pole had dashed as quickly as they could from the Tower, and on reaching the car had thrown their sacks of jewels into the back seat and jumped in behind them, one through each door. Then they waited for the Punk to drive them away, and sat for a few seconds before realizing that he wasn't there, that he wasn't waiting at the steering-wheel — that he was nowhere in sight!

They now decided that one of *them* would have to drive — but couldn't agree on which one!

'*You* drive!' Roly commanded.

'No, *you*,' the Pole insisted.

'No, *you* . . .!'

Eventually the Pole was persuaded that *he* should do the driving, so he had to clamber out of the back seat into the road, and back in again to the driver's seat.

While he was doing this he spotted Super Gran in the distance rushing towards them (with the children lagging behind), and when he looked in the other direction he saw Tub marching the captured Punk along the street. 'Oh-oh! Super Gran!' he yelled, deciding that a fast getaway was called for.

He jumped in and zoomed the car down the road towards Tower Bridge, a few hundred metres away, passing Super Gran, and then the children, on the way.

As they reached the bridge the traffic lights changed to red and bells on the light-standards started to ring, indicating that the bridge was about to be raised to let shipping through beneath it.

But the car managed to shoot across — the last one to do so — and then stopped on the far side. Roly and the Pole got out to crow over their successful escape.

'We did it!' Roly chortled. 'We managed the "big job"!' He hauled his sack of Crown Jewels out of the car and held it aloft — defiantly, proudly, gloatingly.

'*And* we've escaped that there little old Super Gran!' the Pole added, chuckling.

But, on the other side of the bridge, Super Gran had other ideas! She had not been hanging about! She didn't even stop to think about it. She had just jumped over *one* opening bridge – so why not make it *two*?

'Look, Gran!' Willard had shouted, pointing. 'They're gettin' away!'

'Oh no they're not!' she yelled determinedly. 'Watch this . . .!'

And she set off after the crooks, while the children – and especially Edison! – held their breaths.

'No, Super Gran – you can't . . .!' she began. But the little old lady didn't hear her. For she was already half-way to the bridge!

By the time she reached it the warning bells had stopped ringing and the gates had closed, blocking her way. Or at least they *should* have blocked her way. But of course they didn't!

Although they were over two metres high, Super Gran, without pausing for breath or to think about it, leapt up and over them, clearing them easily – to the utter amazement of the pedestrians and the motorists who were now waiting for the gates to open to let them cross the river.

On the other side of the barriers Super Gran didn't falter in her stride. She just kept going, and sprinted over and up the ever-rising roadway on the bridge to leap upwards and outwards over the ever-increasing gap between the two parts of the bridge.

By now Edison, Willard and everyone else in the

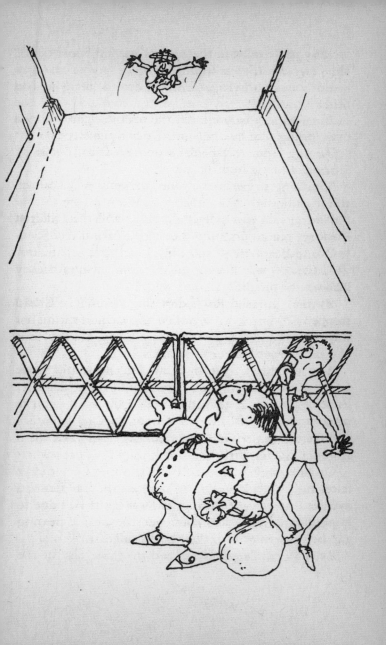

vicinity had rushed to the gates to witness the little old lady leaping like a wizened gazelle across the gap beneath which the River Thames flowed, many metres below.

Super Gran easily cleared the opening gap and was now sliding — on her bottom! — down the slope on the other side, on the bridge's southern half — as it continued rising into the air.

Springing to her feet again, she went into a Super-sprint, followed by another Super-leap as she cleared the barriers on *that* side of the river; and then she put her arms out to grab the waiting, gloating, confident Roly and Beanpole — whose faces had suddenly fallen!

'Got you!' she shouted in triumph as she knocked Roly to the ground. 'I *said* I would!'

'Oh no!' groaned Roly, dropping his sack of Crown Jewels with shock as he rolled away again on his fat little body!

'Oh, but yes!' Super Gran insisted.

'He is a black belt in kung fu,' Roly said when he had stopped rolling and climbed to his feet again, pointing at the Pole, who took up a kung fu stance.

'Havers!' Super Gran retorted. 'The only black belt *he's* got — is that dirty tide-mark round his neck where he never washes!'

'What . . .! Where . . .?' While the baddies distracted themselves by trying to look at the Pole's neck, Super Gran dived forward and grabbed each of them by an arm, twisting it up their backs in an arm-lock.

'Ow! Ouch! Leggo!' screeched the Pole.

'Release me immediately, madam!' demanded Roly, polite to the end!

'Aye, I'll leggo and release you — as soon as I hand you over to the police. Along with those Crown Jewels.'

After the police had taken charge of the crooks — and the jewels — the children joined her, along with Tub, who had also by now got rid of *his* prisoner, the Punk.

'Wow!' Willard enthused, beaming, his eyes gleaming with pride for his favourite old lady, his Gran — his *Super* Gran. 'That was some jump! Terrific! Fantastic! Just like that film on the telly, just like that film . . .' he muttered, over and over like a cracked record!

'Yeah,' Tub agreed, 'it was great! I wish *I* had done it. I bet you I *could* do it . . .!' He glanced longingly at Tower Bridge, hoping that it would swing up again soon and give him the chance!

'Super Gran!' exclaimed Edison, who had taken all this time to recover from the near-faint which the old lady's Super-jump had brought on! 'That was great — but it *was* dangerous, you know! And you *are* an old lady, after all . . .' Edison was a nag, right to the end!

'What?' Super Gran was indignant. 'Me? An old lady?' She was speechless — but not for long! 'Have I got to keep telling you, lassie? I'm Super Gran — and *I* can do . . .'

'*Any*thing!' The three others all finished it for her: Edison, Willard — and Tub.

She grinned. 'Super Gran triumphs once again. Super Gran rules O K! Okay . . .?' She winked.